Tales of Spirit,
Tales of Light

By Arlene Williams

The Waking Light Press
Sparks, Nevada

Printed in the United States of America
on recycled, acid-free paper
using soy ink

Library of Congress Catalog Card Number: 97-90279

Copyright © 1997 by Arlene Williams

All rights reserved. No part of this book may be reproduced or transmitted in any form or by any means, electronic or mechanical, including photocopying, recording or by any information storage and retrieval system—except by a reviewer who may quote brief passages in a review to be printed in a magazine or newspaper—without the written permission of the publisher, except where permitted by law.

Published by:

The Waking Light Press
P. O. Box 1329, Sparks, Nevada 89432

ISBN 0-9605444-6-1

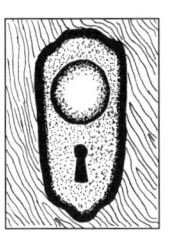 *To Janet,
my sister,
who guided me
to the spiritual door.*

Some Thoughts on Imagining

I call these stories *imaginings*. They are visions born within the creative power of my mind and they are meant to stretch our expectations of what the world could be. They are not to be taken for truth. They are simply to be taken as possibilities. It is from imaginings like these that we can find the inspiration to explore the unknown boundaries of our lives.

For me, imagining is one of the most fundamental processes of human growth. The product of this process, our imaginings, gives us a direction to follow as we recreate our lives each day. I consider this the first step for anyone toward constructive change, for it is only after imagining something new for ourselves that we can begin to make it happen.

These stories are my vision of what I would like to bring forth in my life. I share them in the hope that they may make you think, make you question and encourage you in creating your own.

Table of Contents

Door to the Spirit: Imagination and Perception

The Sapling Girl	2
Great Imaginings	14
The Window Boy	24

Finding the Key: A Loving Heart

The Puppet Master	40
Loving Voices	51
The Earth Witch	63

Stepping Through: Moments of Transformation

Waiting for Dragon	78
A Time of Willingness	89
Mama Eta	98

Beyond the Door: Remembering the Light

Awake Among Whales	112
The Heart of the Dragon	125
The Endless Light	138

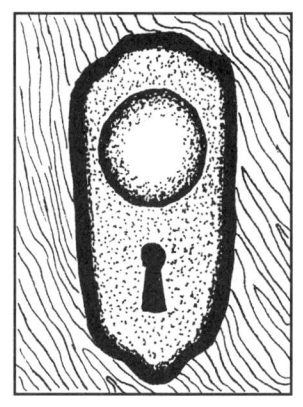

DOOR TO THE SPIRIT:
IMAGINATION AND PERCEPTION

THE SAPLING-GIRL

There once was a time, long ago, when trees had their own special language. It was during this time, in a warm and pleasant land, that one ancient grove of olives found themselves visited, day after day, by a young boy named Damian. He came to sit among the trees and hear the whisper of their leaves as they rustled in the breeze. And as he listened to those long, slow sounds they made, he knew those whispers were words and he wished with all his heart he could understand what they were saying.

As the youngest of four brothers, Damian found life at home very hard. His brothers were strong and brave and gifted in a craft. One brother was apprenticed to a potter, making vases. One brother was apprenticed to a stonemason, building marble temples. And the other brother was just starting out in the village bakery. However, being too young to be apprenticed, Damian could only do chores at home, and the older boys always teased him about it.

"You'll never be a potter," one brother would say. "You couldn't concentrate long enough."

"You'll never be a stonemason," another would say. "You're not strong enough to use a chisel."

The last brother would always remind him, "You're too sloppy to make bread. To make bread you have to measure and be precise."

"I don't care," Damian would reply angrily. Yet though he didn't want to be a baker or a potter or a stonemason, it still hurt to feel so young and useless.

Often Damian would run away and sit in the grove of trees. Sometimes he missed his supper. Sometimes he stayed and camped all night. And though his mother and father always scolded him for being gone, he would explain, "I want to be with trees. I want to grow up and work with them and learn their language."

"But only a sorceress can talk with trees," the others would argue.

"I will learn," Damian would proclaim. "Somehow, I will learn."

One morning, Damian passed through the grove on his way to the meadows to collect willows for his mother's baskets. He stopped for a moment to listen carefully, hoping to understand just one tree groan or rustle or sigh. "Someday," he promised the trees, "I will learn to speak with you." Then he brushed a young sapling lovingly with his fingertips as he went on his way.

It wasn't long before the grove had another visitor—an old and bitter sorceress whose magic was waning. Once, the sorceress had prided herself on her knowledge of the language of trees. However, she couldn't understand their long, slow words anymore. She could only hear the happy rustle of their leaves as they greeted her. That was why, when she sat down to rest in the grove of olives, she decided that they were laughing at her.

"Don't laugh at me!" she scolded the trees as they murmured around her. "And don't whisper, I can't hear what you say."

However, the trees only spoke to her gently, telling her how sad they were that she could not speak with them. And, not understanding what the trees said, the sorceress grew very angry.

"You think I'm old? You think I can't do magic? I can do magic!" she yelled.

The trees were upset. They remembered times when this very sorceress had sat beneath them as a friend, holding long conversations about the world of trees and the world of magic. Now, feeling her fury, they wanted to calm her. So, not knowing what else to do, the trees sent a shower of leaves down around the bent old woman.

The sorceress took it as an insult. "Don't treat me like a fool!" she fumed. "I still have magic. I'll teach you how it feels to be talked about like a nobody." The old woman squinted up her eyes and looked at all the trees with a glare. "Which one shall I pick?"

She walked around the trees studying them. Finally she stopped before the huge twisted trunk of an ancient one. She raised her hand. "Nu. Omega. Oinos," she called.

Nothing happened. The sorceress grunted and raised her hand higher. "Nu! Omega! Oinos!" she yelled as loud as she could.

Again, nothing happened. Then, before admitting defeat, she turned toward the young sapling and raised her hand.

"Nu! Omega! Oinos!" she screeched.

Suddenly a young, girl-like creature stood before her, clothed in a flowing garment of leaves. She stood motionless, with her eyes closed, swaying slightly. The sorceress cackled with glee. "I told you not to fool with me. My magic is very powerful."

Then, as if a rush of wind had filled the grove, all the trees called out to the sapling-girl. They spoke to her with long tree words of dismay, alarmed by the cruel spell the sorceress had put upon her. However the girl did not respond. Like the sorceress, she could not understand the trees. Their words were blurred into a mighty roar that made her feel shivery and frightened.

She could, however, understand the sorceress. "Yes! For a little while, for a day, you will be a nobody," the woman called to her callously as she hobbled on her way.

Alone in the grove, the sapling-girl stood silent, feeling the wind flow through her cloak of leaves. She felt very dizzy, because her roots did not seem to anchor her deep within the ground anymore. Indeed, if she had opened her eyes and looked, she would have seen she had no roots. Like all girls, she had legs and feet to hold her up and move across the ground. But not knowing how to walk, the sapling-girl stayed very, very still for in her heart she was as bound to her spot in the earth as any tree.

The morning passed. The sapling-girl grew weak and lonesome. Without roots to bring water from the soil, her leaves shriveled and began to die. Without lively conversation to nourish her spirit, her heart began to fill with despair. "A nobody," the girl repeated to herself over and over. Having forgotten her own language, those were the only words she could remember to say.

Finally, Damian returned to the grove carrying a bundle of willow sticks from the meadows. He sat down to rest in the shade of the ancient olive and stared at the leaves above him. Then, as he gazed through its gnarled limbs, he heard the rustling voice of the tree call to him urgently. He reached out toward the trunk, not knowing what the words meant. Yet he could feel, through touching the tree, that something was wrong.

Then, as he looked around the grove, his gaze fell on the lovely, thin face of the sapling-girl. Damian jumped to his feet and rushed to her side. He reached out with his hand to shake her arm, thinking she was asleep. "Wake up," he said gently.

The sapling-girl swung her arm away, alarmed by his touch. She swayed violently without her roots to hold her firmly to the ground. Damian grabbed her hand to steady her. She trembled beneath his grip, wondering what had happened to her branches. She could not understand that they had become fingertips. She only knew they now felt bare, no longer covered with bark.

"I'm sorry," he said softly as he let her hand go. "I just wanted to help."

"Help," she echoed in a windy voice. "Help."

"Yes, I'll help," Damian assured her. "But tell me who you are."

"Who you are," the girl echoed. "Who you are."

The boy looked at her mystified, wondering if she was from a foreign land. "I'm Damian. Now who are you? Do you have a name?"

The sapling-girl did not answer. She felt confused by so many words. However, though all the words were new to her, she felt she could understand many of them. "Name," she echoed. "Name."

The boy took her hand and touched his face with it, thinking she must be blind. "Damian," he told her firmly.

"Damian," she echoed.

Then he pressed her hand against her own face. "Name?" he asked.

"Nobody," said the sapling-girl.

Damian shook his head and laughed. "Nobody?"

The sapling-girl nodded, slow and tree-like. "Nobody."

The boy stared at her sadly. Often he felt like a nobody because he wasn't strong or smart or quick like his brothers. Yet, unlike this girl, he could at least see and speak and he knew his own name. He wondered what had happened to this girl to make her act so strange.

"You must be enchanted," he said softly. Then he looked at her lips, so parched and cracked. He realized she was thirsty. He reached for the leather flask that hung over his shoulder. "Some water?" he asked as he opened the flask and poured a drop into her hand.

The sapling-girl nodded vigorously. She reached for the flask and then emptied it at her feet.

"What are you doing?" Damian yelled in amazement.

The girl just shook her head. She was very confused because her roots could not soak up the moisture. "Water," she pleaded. "Water."

Damian shook the flask against her palm. "It's empty," he said with frustration. "We'll have to walk to the spring."

"The spring?" the sapling-girl echoed.

"Yes, in the meadows. I'll lead you there." He tugged her arm slightly.

The sapling-girl dug her heels into the ground as she swayed against his pull.

"Can't you walk?" he asked with exasperation.

The girl shook her head. "Walk?"

Damian stomped his foot. "Oh, why can't you understand?" he shouted with frustration. "Have you never gone anywhere? Have you never moved your legs and walked from one place to another?"

The girl shook her head again and then stood motionless in her same spot.

Damian shrugged. "What can I say? What would make you understand?" he asked with a sigh. Then, knowing she couldn't give him an answer, he touched her shoulder gently. "You wait here. I'll go to the spring."

When Damian returned, he found the girl standing as she had all morning in the middle of the grove with her eyes firmly shut. He watched her for a time, admiring her thick brown hair that flowed over her drooping shoulders. Her face was thin and delicate. Her skin was a light grayish-brown. He looked at her closed eyes, wondering what color they were.

Then he opened the flask and held it to her lips. "Drink," he said as he poured the water gently into her mouth. She swallowed it gratefully, until the whole flask was dry.

And so began a long afternoon, with Damian striving to teach the sapling-girl how to speak his language. He found she didn't comprehend even basic ideas such as eating and working and playing. Yet she loved to sing and her voice was like the gentlest breeze blowing on a summer's day. Damian had never met anyone who knew so little about herself. She truly was nobody.

Finally as twilight fell, Damian urged her to come home with him for her own safety. However she would not move from her spot on the ground.

"Home," she said firmly, pointing to the ground beneath her. "Home."

"You believe you are a tree," Damian decided. Then thinking he might like to fall under the same magic spell, he added, "I would like to be a tree too."

The sapling-girl quivered at that word. "Tree?" she whispered. "Tree?"

"Yes. We're surrounded by trees, but you can't see them. If you could, then you'd know you weren't at all like a tree."

"See?" the girl echoed urgently. "What is see?"

"With your eyes," replied Damian as he touched her eyelid softly.

The girl reached up with her own hand to touch her eyes. Damian suddenly wondered if perhaps she wasn't blind.

"Open them," he whispered.

"Open?" she asked. "What is open?"

"Open…" Damian started, not knowing how to explain to her what it meant. It seemed words were not enough, since she could understand so few. So he took her hand and let her feel how his own eyes opened and shut.

"Yes! Open!" she said and at last her own lids fluttered slightly. Damian was encouraged.

"If you open your eyes you will see the trees," he tempted her.

"Trees," she said with longing. "Trees." And then, slowly, she opened her eyes. She gazed around in the gathering gloom. The massive trunks of olives were right before her. She blinked and looked confused. Then at last she nodded. "Trees," she said pointing to the roots.

Damian reached eagerly for her hand, staring into her deep brown eyes. "Now it's time to walk. See. Look at me. I move my legs to walk."

The sapling-girl stared at the boy before her. She looked at his legs moving back and forth. She shook her head. She pointed to herself. "Tree," she said again and again. "Tree."

"No, you're not a tree. You have no roots. You can walk. If you walk you can touch the trees," pleaded Damian as he pointed to her own legs and feet.

However, the sapling-girl would not look down. Even the promise of touching the trees could not entice her to move. She only watched as Damian walked among the trees, stroking them. Finally Damian gave up and came to her, putting his arm around her shoulder.

"If you won't walk, I'll pick you up and carry you there," the boy said quickly as he gathered her in his arms. Suddenly he felt her fingernails tearing at his face.

"No!" the girl screamed as her feet were pulled from the ground. "No!"

She thrashed her arms about like limbs tossing wildly in a storm. Damian ignored her, determined to get her to a tree. He struggled forward burying his face into her cloak of leaves so she could not scratch him. Then, as Damian brushed against the rough bark of an olive, the girl grew still. Damian looked up, realizing she had fainted.

Again and again, Damian tried to wake her as, inside, a strange feeling grew. He knew he had been wrong to take her away from that patch of ground she had clung to. Finally, he rushed back to it with the girl in his arms, his heart pulsing with panic.

He laid her on the ground and groped in the early evening darkness, hoping to feel the footprints she had left in the damp earth so he could stand her up exactly where she had been. To his amazement, he found not footprints, but a hole in the ground that branched out into narrow channels as if some young and tender roots had been wrenched from the soil.

Then, feverishly, he planted the girl's feet back into the hole, pressing the soft dirt around her legs till they were firmly in place and couldn't move. Finally he lifted her limp, unconscious body and helped her stand as straight and tall as he could.

"Wake up. Wake up," he whispered again and again. "You are no longer nobody. You're a tree."

After several moments, the girl began to move. "Home," she murmured happily. "Home."

Damian nodded with pleasure as he stroked her long brown hair. "Yes, you're back home, my precious tree."

She smiled at him and then she sang to Damian her loveliest song yet.

The next morning Damian woke beside a young olive sapling freshly planted in the ground. He smiled at the beautiful young tree. He had no memory of exactly when he fell asleep. Yet he vaguely remembered talking to someone in words that were strange and long and whispering.

His heart leapt. Even if he could not recall what was said, he had, at last, spoken to a tree. Somehow, he knew he would find a way to learn more. Then, perhaps, his dream of spending his life working with trees could come true.

He reached for the sapling and touched its leaf. A word came on the wind. It was rhythmic and gentle, yet firm.

Damian smiled, wondering what it meant. Then he heard the tree word again. Its music flowed inside him and he realized he had heard that same word the night before. He searched his mind for its meaning. Then he remembered, all at once, what that one long word meant. In the language of the trees, it meant: *I will teach you.*

Damian smiled at the young tree. He pushed some stray bits of soil, loosened the night before, firmly against its roots. Then he sat quietly, waiting with great patience for the next word to come. Finally a word rustled in the breeze, soft and gentle.

Damian knew at once what the word meant. He looked at the young olive sapling, remembering the day they had shared. Then he repeated the tree word as best he could with a soft, hushed whisper, adding to himself with a nod, "Yes, little tree. Yes. We are friends."

GREAT IMAGININGS

Long ago, during a great and terrible war, a young girl was sent to live with her uncle and his family in their country stronghold. Azura did not want to go there. She protested loudly at being sent away, but her parents believed she would be safer in a sturdy stone fortress far from the fighting. To Azura it sounded like a forlorn and desolate place to live—alone, without her friends or her parents. Her mother assured her, though, that she would not be lonely because her cousin Rekee was her very same age.

She arrived one morning, full of dismal expectations. As she had feared, Uncle Tren's land was totally isolated. It lay in the middle of a dark forest filled with sounds that were strange to a village girl. The fortress itself was large with fields, an orchard, a huge chicken coop and a small herd of cows within its walls. Uncle Tren, Aunt Narah and the servants were kept endlessly busy tending the animals and the crops. That was why, after a quick hug and hello, Azura found herself left in the care of her cousin Rekee.

It wasn't long till Azura realized that Rekee was the strangest girl she had ever met. Rekee hummed to herself as she ate her meals and often took minutes to answer a simple question. When she did, the words she spoke seemed to trail off into nowhere. She would walk down the corridors of the main house, stopping at a shadow, peering into it as if she could see something there. And everyday Rekee wandered out into the forest alone.

Azura knew she did, because she would watch from her chamber window as Rekee disappeared through a little door in the orchard wall. Azura always spent the day quietly, sometimes reading, sometimes painting, sometimes waiting in the orchard for Rekee to return. When her cousin finally came back through the door, Azura would ask her where she had been. Rekee always stared dreamily at the tree tops and answered simply, "I went... I went... ah, yes... I went imagining."

One morning, Azura secretly followed her through the door into the forest. She found Rekee sitting on the bank of a small stream, staring straight ahead. Azura crouched behind a fallen tree, watching her. However Rekee seemed to be doing nothing and Azura grew restless.

Just as Azura was about to return to the fortress, she heard Rekee say very slowly and deliberately, "Tail. Long tail. Spiny tail. Scales. Foot. Claws."

Rekee paused. Then she began again, "Tail. Long tail. Spiny tail. Shiny scales. Large foot. Claws." Rekee stopped once more and waited. Nothing happened for a moment. Then, in front of her, there appeared—like a giant reflection rippling through the air—a long, silver tail and one foot with

sharp, curved claws.

Azura blinked her eyes, not understanding what was lingering, mist-like, before her eyes. A moment later, it was gone and Azura ran back, in alarm, to the door in the orchard wall.

Hastily she climbed the narrow stairs to her bedroom chamber and stayed there most of the day, agonizing over Rekee's secret. She wanted to tell someone about it, yet she half-feared if she told her aunt and uncle, she would discover they already knew. If Narah's and Tren's ways were just as strange as Rekee's, Azura preferred to stay ignorant of it. So, she watched out her window, wondering when her cousin would return.

It was almost dusk when Rekee slipped back through the little door. Azura watched her stare dreamily at an apple on a tree branch, then pass through the orchard toward the dining hall.

Realizing it was suppertime and she was hungry, Azura gathered her courage and descended the stairs quickly. She ran along the dark, narrow corridors of the fortress, uneasy at being alone. When she entered the brightly lit hall, she felt relieved, but as she passed Rekee's dusty cloak, cast over an empty chair, she noticed an acrid smell like smoke.

At the table, the conversation was minimal. Narah looked ashen as she ate. Rekee's father hardly touched his food. Finally, as the girls ate their cake, Tren turned to them and said, "The fighting is coming close. It is too dangerous to leave the fortress grounds. You can play within the orchard, but that is all."

Azura turned to her cousin, looking for a reaction to the news, but Rekee just nodded vacantly.

The next morning, Azura watched the little wooden door,

wondering if Rekee would go through it. Soon she saw her cousin wander into the orchard. However Rekee didn't go near the door. Instead, she sat in the center of the orchard and stared at the ivy covered wall. "Eyes," she called. "Red eyes. Fiery eyes. Blazing hot like coals."

Azura held her breath as her cousin continued, "Huge eyes. Deep eyes. Burning with power." Like the vision yesterday, the image of those eyes, which Rekee was summoning now, appeared in the air before her.

Shuddering at the sight of those two fierce eyes, Azura closed the shutters to her window and cowered within her room all day. She asked for her meals to be brought to her. However, after a few days in her chambers, Azura felt she couldn't live without some company and some exercise. So she left her room, vowing to avoid Rekee as much as was possible.

Rekee wandered the halls these days, mumbling softly to herself, "The fighting is coming close… very close."

Azura shook her head at her cousin. She supposed it was worry over the war that made Rekee act so strange. Still Rekee's terrible secret was more than a product of someone's fearful imagination. Azura had seen those fiery eyes.

Often Azura would catch a word, uttered in the corridor ahead of her, like *ears* or *teeth* or *jaws*. And once, when Rekee passed Azura's open doorway, Azura shivered as if something lurked nearby that she couldn't see. It was like a faint shimmer in Rekee's shadow as Azura looked from the corner of her eye.

Azura would always head for the orchard, when Rekee was wandering the halls, hoping her cousin would not follow her there. But as Azura walked among the plums and the pears, everything around her seemed tainted by the lingering smell of smoke.

One evening, as Azura walked in the orchard, listening to the call of a night bird, she heard voices beyond the wall. There were men there, speaking in a language strange to her. She knew instantly, they were soldiers and they were not her own.

She froze as something rammed against the little wooden door. A board splintered and the door was rammed again. Then, before she could turn to flee, Rekee was standing beside her calling calmly, "Tail. Long tail. Spiny tail. Huge feet. Sharp claws."

Azura looked at her bewildered. She felt a prickle of goose bumps on her skin. Then, as a soldier burst through the broken door, Rekee pointed above the wall. "Silver scales. Strong back. Neck stretching across the sky."

Men poured into the orchard and surrounded them. Rekee didn't flinch. She just raised her voice louder. "Ears. Teeth. Blazing eyes."

One of the soldiers stepped forward, pointing his sharp sword at them. Rekee called with all her might, "Wings! Fire! Roar!"

All at once, wind gusts rustled the trees in the orchard and the forest beyond. Air rushed over them, like a giant wing was beating. The smell of smoke filled the air. The soldiers looked around anxiously.

Then Azura heard it. It started as a low rumble. It grew stronger and stronger. Some soldiers retreated toward the door. Azura could almost see those fiery red eyes in the air above them.

Rekee touched Azura's hand. "Shine!" Rekee called. "Shine! Shimmer! Shine!"

Suddenly, there it was—a dragon, fifty feet long and

gleaming silver, with hot-coal eyes. The soldiers ran from the orchard, through the broken door. Azura just stared at the creature, which hovered for a moment in its translucent way. Then it disappeared bit by bit. First the wings. Then the eyes. Then the scales and teeth and tail. Finally the last claw faded into the orchard twilight.

After a long silence, Rekee turned to Azura. "It was one of my imaginings," she explained.

Azura looked at her cousin in wonder. She no longer feared Rekee, for at last she understood her cousin's strange ways. "It was a great one, to be sure," Azura said with deep respect.

Rekee nodded dreamily. "I've been practicing."

"I would like to imagine, too," Azura said, hopefully. "Will you teach me?"

Rekee studied her with a steady gaze. Finally she shook her head and laughed. "Don't you know how to imagine?"

"Yes, but not like you."

"Close your eyes... and... picture the dragon," Rekee instructed, searching for the words carefully.

Azura closed her eyes.

"Do you see it?"

Azura nodded.

"Picture it strong... again and again... everyday." Rekee shrugged. "Till it begins to happen."

That night, as she stared out her chamber window at the stars, Azura held within her mind the vision of the shimmering dragon. She started with the eyes, focusing her mind on them. Then she searched the night sky for any sign of eyes, glowing hot like coals. There wasn't any. Finally she gave up. She crawled into her bed, deciding that Rekee had a special gift she could never have. She fell asleep, listening to the workmen sealing up the doorway in the orchard wall with stone.

The next morning, Rekee was in the orchard inspecting the new stonework on the wall. "Are you sad?" Azura asked her softly.

Rekee looked up in her dreamy way. "No time for that." She stared into the walnut tree above her. "I have... I have a new imagining. You can help me."

Azura shook her head. "I'm no good. I tried last night. I couldn't even get the eyes to appear."

"One night?" Rekee laughed as she watched an ant climb across the bark of the tree. "Months..." she said softly. "It takes months... or years."

"Years?" Azura frowned.

Rekee nodded. "I have a new imagining..." she repeated. Then she sat down and patted the ground beside her. "Help me."

"How?" asked Azura as she sat beside her cousin.

"Last night," Rekee began slowly, "as the men ran away... I knew they could come back." Rekee picked up a spider crawling across her skirt and examined it carefully for a moment. Then she continued, "Next time the dragon might not be enough."

Azura nodded in alarm. "Perhaps two dragons would. If I practiced hard, two dragons would scare them away."

Rekee shook her head. "Not another dragon... no... there is something else to imagine." Rekee spread her arms wide, as if she were trying to encompass the whole orchard. "Something greater."

"There is?"

"Yes." Rekee smiled happily. "More powerful... more powerful than a dragon could ever be."

Azura shook her head. "I don't understand. What is it?"

Rekee looked at Azura with joyful eyes. She took a very deep breath. Finally she answered simply, "Peace."

"I don't understand," Azura repeated. "How do you imagine peace?"

Rekee stared at the wall where the door used to be. "A vision... a song... or a feeling," she answered carefully.

Azura nodded slowly. "I can imagine a peaceful feeling. Is that what you mean?"

Rekee took her cousin's hand and squeezed it. "We must begin." Then she closed her eyes and said clearly, calling in her powerful way, "Peace. In the orchard. In the hallways. In the fortress. Everywhere."

Azura stared all around her, waiting for something to appear. However, she saw no claws or eyes or smoke. There was, however, the song of a bird and the buzz of a bee and a gentle breeze filling her with stillness. Azura smiled, closing her eyes too. She took a deep breath and added simply, "In my heart... peace."

It was months later, on a crisp autumn day, that Rekee and Azura sat on a hill overlooking a broad plain filled with people. They were far from the fortress for they had traveled for a day and a night after begging Rekee's father to take them there.

Two armies were spread across the plain and in the center a long procession of horses and carriages came toward the hillside slowly and majestically. Finally the procession stopped and a woman stepped out of one carriage. She wore a long purple robe with a heavy crown. She was the ruler of the enemy kingdom. A man stepped out from another carriage. He wore a white robe studded with jewels. He was the ruler of Azura's land.

As they watched, both girls focused on something in their heart. It was warm and joyful, yet quiet and calm. It was the feeling that they had imagined everyday, now, for such a long time. They let it build and flow out of them like a wave washing down the hillside.

The woman reached out her hand, offering a rolled parchment. The man took it gladly with a respectful bow. Then together they walked toward the hillside and spoke to the crowd, which cheered wildly. Azura and Rekee could not hear the words they said, but they didn't need to.

Both girls smiled. "Peace," they whispered softly, calling it forth. "In the people. In the kingdom. Everywhere."

And all around them they could feel the echo of that peace.

THE WINDOW BOY

Once upon a time, an old church stood at a forgotten mountain crossroads. Inside, empty pews were neatly arranged before the altar. The church was vacant, but it was still decorated with sacred treasures. The people of the parish, though, had long since vanished. Now, only spiders and mice found any reason to congregate inside the gray stone walls of the church.

It was to this church that a young shepherd found his way during a treacherous April storm. Dellon had strayed too far from his hut looking for a lost lamb. Then, as an icy sleet came pouring down, he fought his way through the freezing winds to the door of a building. Pushing it open, he found himself surrounded by spider webs inside a gloomy room that echoed with mystery. He realized, by the pews, he was in a church and, feeling comforted by that, curled up to sleep.

When he opened his eyes again, he was met with a brilliant chorus of color, splashing the walls of the church all around him. Startled, he sat up with a jolt, searching the vaulted ceilings for a clue as to where the colors came from. Soon enough, he realized the sun was shining through a stained glass window behind the altar. Its reds and greens and golds penetrated the dusty air with strong shafts of light.

Dellon stared at it, feeling as if the colors were penetrating not just the room but himself. It was a simple window with only a recurring pattern of circles and lines to weave its spell of color. And yet that pattern, like the intricate webs all around him, was absolutely beautiful.

The shepherd sat, mesmerized by the window. He wished there was someone he could tell of the wonderful spell it cast over him. He wanted to describe the pattern of colors and the feelings inside him. However, being a shepherd boy, he lived alone with the sheep, and he never had anyone with whom to share.

Dellon moved beyond the dusty pews, up the center aisle and past the altar. He didn't even notice the gold chalice or the gem-studded candlesticks which graced the altar cloth. His complete attention was on the window. He reached out with his hand and touched the blaze of light in front of him. For a moment he was enchanted by its colors against his skin. And then, as he studied the leaded glass, he saw them.

There were three of them—all boys, all a deep yellow color—moving slowly through a thick golden circle. They were very tiny, and rather stretched out by the flatness of the glass. Dellon would have missed them, except he could hear them speaking.

"We're almost there," one was saying in a hollow monotone.

"Hurry then," scolded another with a voice that was just as flat. "I can't stand to be golden much longer."

"I'm tired," whined the third. Dellon recognized him as younger than the other ones. His voice was higher and richer. It seemed he could speak in two notes and not just one.

"Oh hush, Tarrie," complained the first. "I can feel the edge of the gold. Next will be red. I know it. It'll be red."

"Go on without me," Tarrie muttered. "I don't want to be red."

"Come on," urged the first. "We can't leave you."

"Oh, leave him," grumbled the second. "Mother and Father will find him. They're somewhere behind."

"You'll have to wait for them here," warned the first boy as he rose from the golden glass to clamber over the thick gray leading that separated each section of the window. For a moment, the boy lost his golden color and regained a round, thick shape. Then as his slipped into the red of the next piece of glass he flattened out again—his face, now, bright scarlet.

The second boy followed, leaving Tarrie alone in the golden circle. The window boy turned slowly toward Dellon, then stared past him as if he were nothing. It wasn't until Dellon moved his finger that he looked closely at the shepherd's hand.

"Hello," Dellon greeted him.

The window boy continued staring at his hand.

"Can't you hear me?" Dellon inquired as he wiggled his finger back and forth.

The boy followed the movement with his eyes, saying nothing. At last he spoke, "I can hear you. Somehow, I can hear you. But where are you?"

Dellon was surprised at his question. "Don't you know?

I'm out here beyond the window."

Suddenly Tarrie smiled. "I knew it. There is a place beyond the window."

Dellon giggled with amazement. "Of course there is. That's where my finger is. You watched it move."

"Yes, I saw your finger move," Tarrie chanted in his hollow way. He looked beyond the finger and up the arm to Dellon's face. His eyes grew wide with excitement. "They always told me there was nothing beyond the window. I never believed it," the window boy explained.

"How many people live in this window?" Dellon asked as he stared at the other two boys, moving slowly through the red toward a section of green.

"There are five in my family," Tarrie replied, "my parents, my brothers and me." Then the boy stared through the golden glass at the big empty room of the church. "How many people live beyond the window?"

"Oh, many more than five." Dellon laughed. "I couldn't tell you how many."

"But where are they?"

Dellon stared at the boy, wondering how to explain the world to him. "This is just an empty building," he finally began. "It's called a church. But beyond the church there is something more. It's called the world and it's so big it seems to never end."

"Never end?" the window boy mumbled flatly. "How could it never end?"

"Come out of the glass and I'll show you," Dellon urged.

Tarrie wagged his stretched out head from side to side, forlornly. "Come out of the glass? I can't. I'm trapped."

"But you move from color to color," the shepherd protested. "You can do the same thing. Just come out of the gold

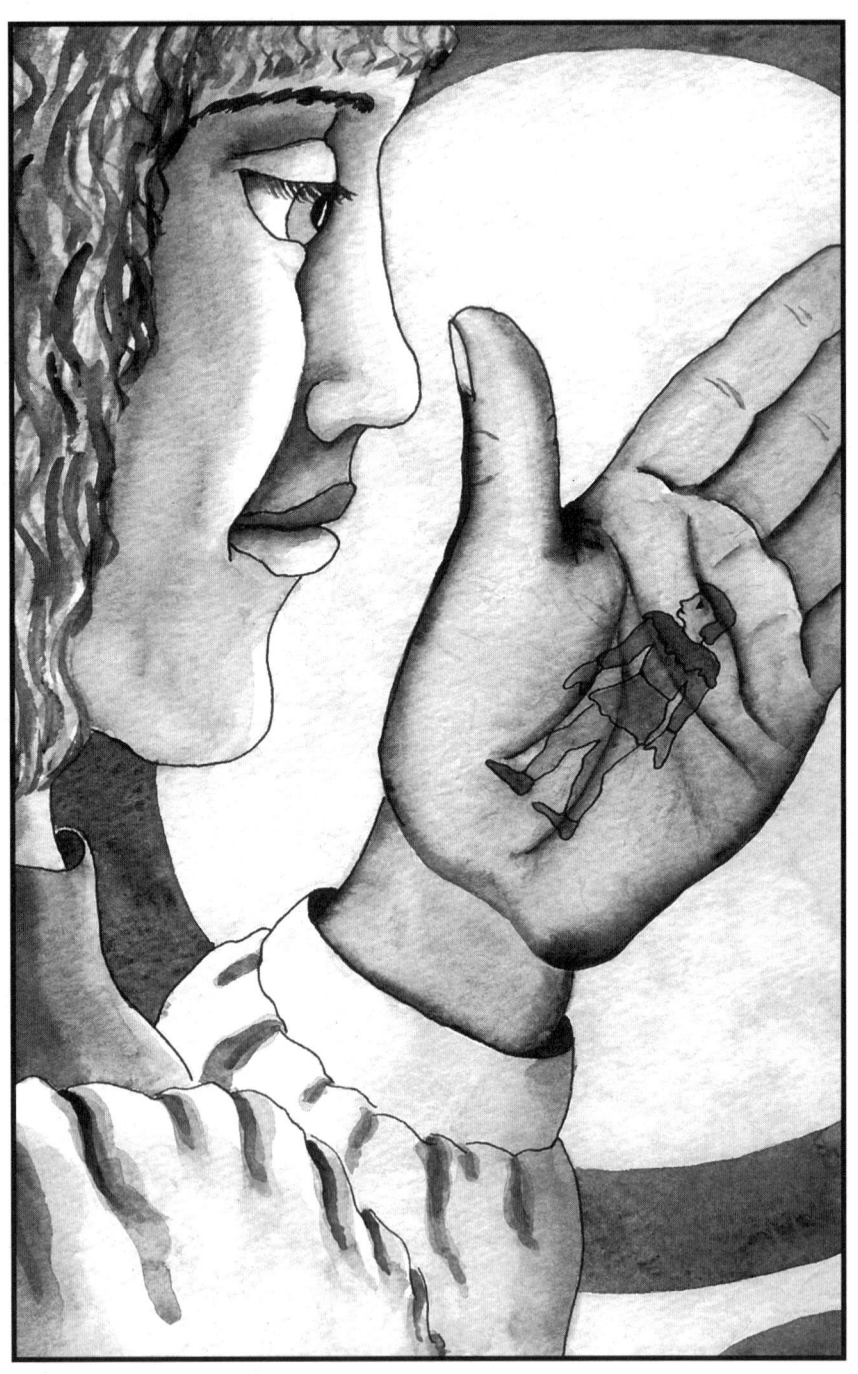

but don't go back into the red."

There was a long silence as the window boy thought over what Dellon had said. Finally he agreed, "Yes, just don't go back in. I never considered that."

"I'll hold out my hand," Dellon suggested. "Then you won't fall."

"Fall?" Tarrie wondered.

"Once you're out of the window, you'll find out," Dellon assured him.

And so Tarrie moved slowly through the golden circle to the gray leading surrounding it. Carefully he emerged from the glass. Then as he clung to the leading he looked at the fingers reaching toward him. Quickly he stepped onto the shepherd's palm, standing proud and three-dimensional. "I did it!" he yelled in a full, rich voice. "I did it!"

However, a moment later he suddenly melted into Dellon's hand.

"What happened?" Dellon cried as he stared at the flat boy on the palm of his hand. Tarrie shrugged. Dellon could feel the tickle of that movement through his skin. "You're part of me," he whispered in amazement.

"Part of you?"

"Yes, you are inside my hand somehow."

"Your hand is not the world?" Tarrie asked sadly.

Dellon shook his head, then added brightly. "But from my hand you can see the world."

"Oh, yes," the window boy called to him. "Take me to see the world."

And so, Dellon burst from the forgotten church into the brightness of spring. He spent the morning showing Tarrie the mountain meadows and the tall trees. He took him to the edge of a cliff so he could see the valleys stretched out before them. Tarrie loved the white of the clouds and the blue of the sky and the purple of the lupines for those were colors he had never seen before. But most of all he loved the shepherd's sheep.

"They can move, like you move," the window boy exclaimed.

"Yes," Dellon sighed, remembering the lost lamb. "Sometimes they move where they shouldn't." He told his new friend about losing the lamb.

All at once the window boy laughed. "I'm lost too. Mother and Father could never find me here beyond the window."

"They will be frightened for you."

"Oh, they won't know." Tarrie shook his head. "They could never imagine me going anywhere except from red to gold to green. They won't be frightened."

"But is that all they do?" asked Dellon.

Tarrie grinned. "Yes. They love the colors of the glass—except for the gray between them. Mother never let me be gray, only red and gold and green."

"How can they tolerate it day after day?"

"I don't know. But I'm so tired of it. This is much better. Still…" The window boy paused and looked up at his new friend. "Still, I wish I could stand free like you."

"I don't understand why you can't." Dellon shrugged. "For a moment you stood free, when you stepped onto my hand. You just can't stay that way. Perhaps you need to be part of something."

All the rest of the day Dellon showed off his shepherd's world to the tiny window boy. It was great to have the company but he felt sorry for his little friend. He wondered how he would feel if he could not walk or run or stand tall and free. And yet there was something about the window boy that made him feel a touch of envy. The window boy was always part of something—not like a shepherd, forever alone.

That night was cold in the shepherd's hut and Dellon was careful to keep his hand beneath his sheepskin covers in case the window boy would feel the cold. He dreamed many wonderful dreams of exploring the world with his new friend and woke at dawn feeling happy. However, his happiness did not last long. For when he looked at his palm to say hello, he found the window boy had vanished.

Dellon ate his oats sadly and went out to tend the sheep. It wasn't till late afternoon that he came back inside the hut and started a fire to cook his beans. Then as he was stirring the beans in the pot, he noticed something move on the clay wash basin beside him. Dellon jumped with surprise and delight. It was the window boy.

Dellon sighed with relief. "I thought I had lost you. How did you get there?" he asked as he peered closely at his tiny friend moving slowly through the red-brown bowl.

"I just moved from thing to thing. I wanted to explore on my own, while you slept," Tarrie explained.

"Don't you sleep?"

"Only when I'm bored," the window boy explained. "Here, I could never be bored."

Dellon dished up his beans. "Do you eat?" he asked his guest.

"I don't know. What is eat?"

"This," Dellon explained as he swallowed a spoonful of beans.

"Isn't that strange," said Tarrie with wonder as the food disappeared. "I become a part of things. You make things a part of you."

"Well, not everything," Dellon mumbled as he chewed. "Only food."

"Oh, I wish I could eat, too," Tarrie said softly. "You are so lucky, Dellon."

Dellon stared at his beans. It felt rude to eat in front of his new friend. "Perhaps I should stop."

"No! No!" Tarrie insisted. So Dellon continued and the window boy found each bite absolutely fascinating.

When his meal was done, Dellon poured some warm water into the basin to wash his dishes. But before he could, he found his little friend gently rocking back and forth on the surface of the water. The water made him look rounder.

"Oh, Dellon!" the window boy cried. "What is this? It is delightful." Then he added with joy, "And look, it doesn't make me quite so flat."

Dellon smiled. "It's water," he answered simply.

"Water is wonderful," Tarrie said with satisfaction. "It's like you. It moves."

After the dishes were done, Dellon took Tarrie out to check on the sheep. Tarrie moved within the threads of Dellon's coat, eager to look out on the shadows of moonlight all around him.

"I like the night," Dellon whispered to the window boy as he counted his sheep. "When it's night, I don't feel so alone. For an instant, I can imagine the darkness around me, connecting me to everything. It must be how you feel all the time."

"What is alone?" Tarrie whispered back.

"Alone is..." Dellon struggled to explain. "Alone is apart. Separate. Not connected to anything."

"But that's what I want," Tarrie insisted. "It must be so great to move freely on your own."

"Not always," Dellon admitted. "Sometimes it is nice to feel connected to something or someone. If you're not, you feel lonely."

"I see," said Tarrie slowly. "It is not only me, then, that must be part of something."

Later, as Dellon lay down to sleep, he called to Tarrie quietly in the darkness, "Please be careful, my little friend. Don't wander too far. I would not want to lose you, ever."

"I promise," Tarrie assured him. "I will stay close. I will not leave you alone."

"Thank you," Dellon answered with gratitude. Then, as he closed his eyes and fell asleep, a warm glow filled his heart. And he dreamed all night of flying hand in hand with Tarrie, through a star filled sky.

The next morning, when he woke, the first thing he did was call out to the window boy. "Tarrie. What a wonderful dream I had. Come. Let me tell you."

However, the shepherd's hut was silent. Dellon jumped from his cot and opened the door. "Tarrie!" he called frantically. "Tarrie!"

There was no answer.

Dellon searched all around the hut. No small voice greeted him. Then as he went outside to tend the sheep, Dellon felt the loneliness of the shepherd's life fill him once again.

Dellon stayed close to the sheep all morning. At least the sheep filled the air with noisy bleats and sometimes nuzzled him. However, he couldn't forget the window boy and he found himself wondering what it would be like to move through glass and clay and thread. Then he remembered how Tarrie had tickled the palm of his hand and was amazed that someone else had been a part of him.

Dellon ate his lunch of cheese and bread beneath a

grand oak tree. Then he closed his eyes and leaned back against the trunk, thinking of the sap inside rising with the spring and the leaves getting ready to unfurl. Trees had always been such a wonderful mystery to him. He wished he was Tarrie now, sinking into the strong, hard wood.

All afternoon, Dellon followed the sheep as they grazed along the edge of a stream. Then as he sat on the bank and dipped his hand through the water, he saw again, in his mind, the window boy floating in the water of the clay basin. He looked at his hand, surrounded by the cool wetness of the creek. "I am part of something," he said, startled. "I am like Tarrie in the water. I am part of it."

It wasn't till the gloom of twilight spread over him, that he realized the true gift that the window boy had given him. It started with the sunset and a golden alpine glow washing over him. As he watched the color of his hand change with the setting sun, he remembered Tarrie's golden face the first time they had met. For one brief moment, Dellon imagined the air, thick like glass, and himself a window boy, moving through it. Then as the twilight gray took over, and he felt the comforting cloak of darkness near, he whispered, "I am a part of everything."

Yes, the twilight darkness, like the water, did surround him, making him a part of everything. He had imagined that often, but had never really believed it. Now, even though he could not move through wood and stone and glass like the window boy, he could feel a nearness to the rest of the world he had never felt before. He was not separate or alone at all.

Dellon stood there in the shadows, soaking up that closeness to the trees and the sheep and the mountain he lived upon. The sheep felt gentle in his heart, the trees wise. The mountain held ancient wordless secrets that lingered in his mind. He saw a star appear in the sky. Like in his dream, he knew the distance was not too great between them. Somehow, a part of him could touch that star.

Then he heard a small voice being blown to him on the evening breeze. "Dellon! Dellon! Catch me! Here I come. Catch me!" the window boy called.

Not seeing anything, Dellon could only raise his hands wildly, thinking his friend was falling from the trees above. Then as the wind moved through his hands, the window boy appeared there, clinging breathlessly to his finger.

"Oh, Tarrie, I've missed you so," Dellon gasped. He lowered his hand and let Tarrie stand upon it. "And look at you. You're standing free! What happened?"

"It was you. You gave me the answer when you talked about the night," the window boy said breathlessly. "It made me think of the gray color between the glass and how mother hated that color so. She taught us to always step over the gray instead of moving through it." Tarrie grinned at his friend and continued. "I started to think, as you slept, that maybe the night was like a very dark gray and I could just step out into it, too. So I tried and I did. I still feel part of something, but rounder, like in the water."

"Better than in the water. You don't look flat at all. But where were you?" asked Dellon with concern. "I looked for you all day."

"When I stepped out into the night, it moved. I did not know it could move so fast," Tarrie said in awe.

"That's the wind blowing," Dellon explained.

"Well, first it took me down the mountain, and then it took me up. And now tonight it began to take me down again. I'm so glad you caught me. I was getting quite dizzy."

Dellon burst out laughing at his vision of his little friend, blown about in the breeze. "It's like the dream I had last night," he chuckled. "We were both flying in the starry sky."

"Oh, yes," Tarrie urged. "Come with me. Fly on the wind!"

"I can't," Dellon said with a smile. "I'm too big. The wind cannot blow me."

"Really? Your dream cannot come true?" Tarrie asked sadly.

"Not in that way," Dellon answered thoughtfully. "But in another way it can. We are friends and our friendship connects us. When you fly on the wind, in my heart I fly with you," Dellon declared triumphantly.

"Yes, yes!" the window boy danced in circles on Dellon's hand. Then he stopped and said soberly, "But not tonight. I've seen enough of the world for one day, and I have something more important to do."

"What?" Dellon asked hopefully. "What do you have to do?"

Tarrie hugged Dellon's thumb, very hard. "Spend some time with a friend, a very close friend," he said gently. "You."

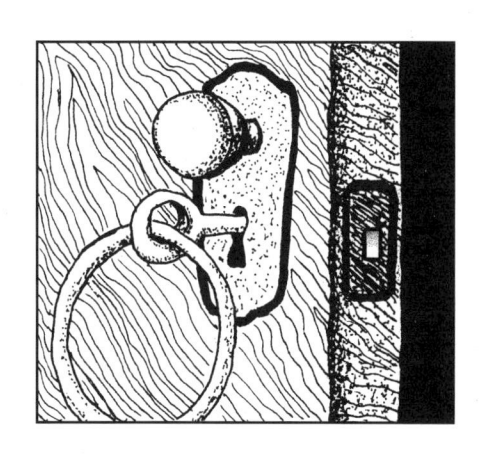

FINDING THE KEY:
A LOVING HEART

THE PUPPET MASTER

There once was a boy who longed to be a puppeteer like his Grandfather. He loved the feeling of pulling a string and making a puppet come to life. He loved deciding whether the arm should move up or the leg should move down or the head should move from side to side. And especially, he loved the idea that he was the puppet's master—the one in charge.

His name was Simon and he spent every summer with his cousins in the small thatched cottage of his grandparents. Since he had no brothers or sisters, his mother hoped he would learn to get along with other children by spending part of the year living in a house full of them. However, Simon did not learn at all.

Every morning, unless it rained, Simon's grandmother would shoo all the children out of the cottage to play for the day. For the first hour things would go fine. Eventually, though, Simon would yell at someone because they wouldn't follow him when he was the leader or play tag the way he wanted. He always demanded an extra turn, no matter what the game; and usually, if he didn't win the foot race, he'd pout. Then, in a huff, Simon would slip back inside the cottage to play alone with Grandfather's puppets and pretend he was a great puppet master.

"I see you love the puppets," Grandfather said one morning when he found Simon inside, alone.

"Yes." Simon smiled shyly.

"I've always loved the puppets too," Grandfather said softly. "I remember when I was your age, my aunt gave me my first marionette. I practiced with her everyday till I could make her move so smoothly that she seemed real. Perhaps it's time to give that marionette to you."

"You still have it?" Simon asked breathlessly, trembling at the thought of owning one of Grandfather's puppets.

"Yes, she is my most cherished puppet," Grandfather said slowly. "Do you think you can treat her well?"

Simon nodded enthusiastically.

"We shall see," said Grandfather with a twinkle in his eye. "If you treat her well this summer, I will let you take her home for keeps. If you don't, I will save her for another grandchild."

Simon's mouth dropped open earnestly. "I will take good care of her," he promised. "You will see."

"Very well," said Grandfather as he walked to a trunk and raised the lid. Very carefully he pulled out a beautiful marionette ballerina dressed in silver slippers and a flowing blue dress.

"Her name is Lorette," he said reverently as he unwound the strings from the wooden cross piece that held them. "If you treat her well, she will dance for you as no puppet you've seen before."

Grandfather gently began to work the strings. Lorette raised her arm and turned her head sideways. The puppet stood up on pointed toes and steadied herself. Slowly she began to turn and dip in an ordinary puppet-like way. Grandfather smiled patiently as he watched the marionette. "She's warming up," he explained.

Then, as Simon began to doubt that this puppet was special at all, Lorette leaped high into the air. In a moment she was gliding and spinning so gracefully, she could have been a famous ballerina dancing on a miniature stage. She did a perfect pirouette, then leaned forward, balancing delicately on one leg as still as a crane. Simon watched her, spellbound, as Lorette twirled away across the table and back again. Her kicks were smooth and powerful. Her jumps precise, and her body flowed effortlessly with each movement. All too soon the performance was over.

"Here," Grandfather said as he handed Simon the strings. "I will leave you with Lorette."

Grandfather left the room and Simon eagerly picked up the strings. He raised Lorette onto her toes, working the strings carefully. Lorette raised her arm stiffly and curtsied awkwardly. She took a few clumsy steps forward on her toes then tumbled into a limp heap. "Puppet!" Simon commanded. "I am your master. You must dance."

Simon raised the puppet again and worked the strings deliberately to make the puppet leap and turn. The puppet did as the strings instructed, but nothing magical happened. She did not dance as she had for his grandfather. Simon scratched his head and frowned. "You must dance. I want you to dance," he scolded the puppet.

All day, Simon worked with the puppet trying over and

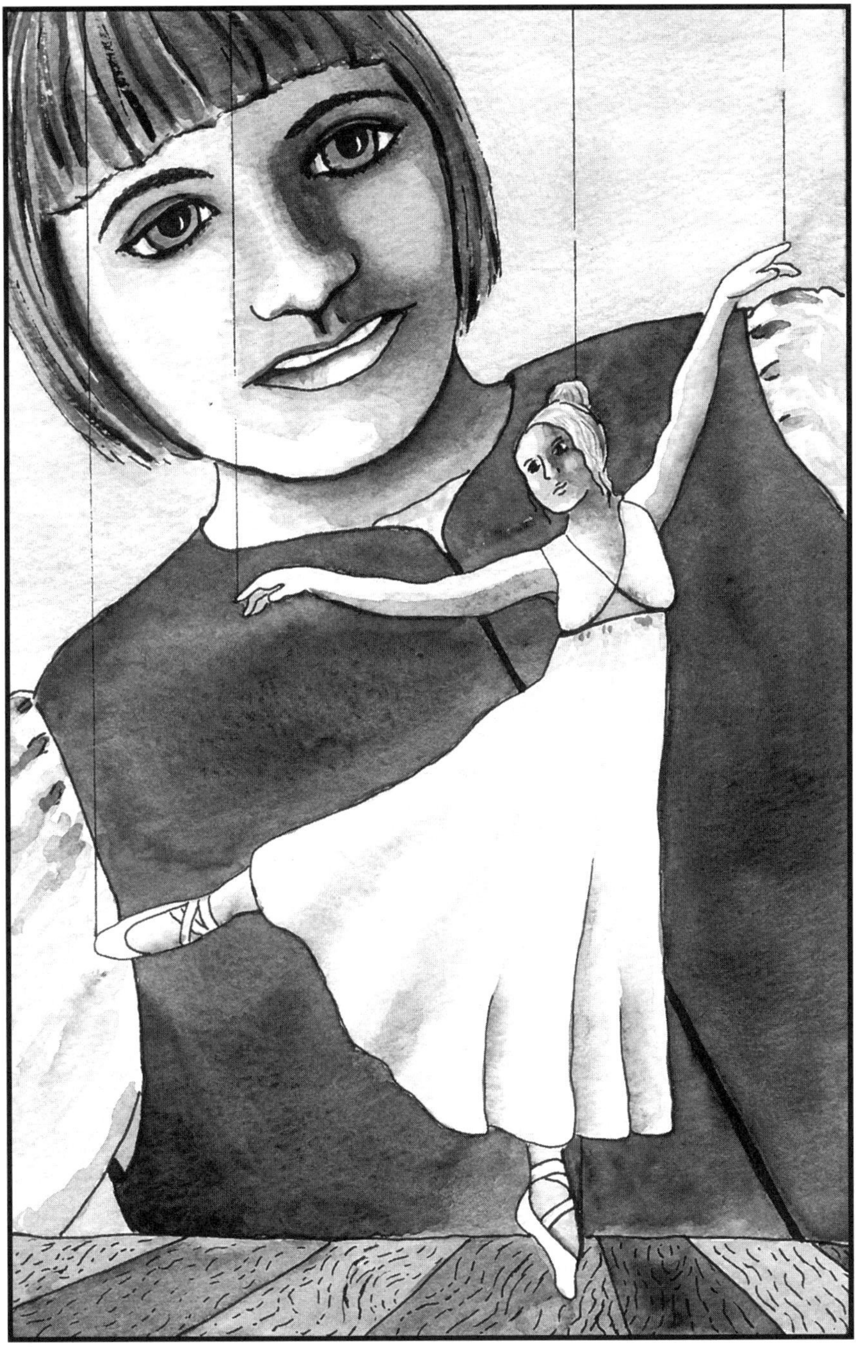

over to make her dance. Often he threw the marionette down in frustration, only to pick her up quickly, worried that Grandfather would catch him. He was determined to keep the puppet for his own, yet this little wooden toy was quickly becoming the most maddening thing he had ever encountered. And though he threatened and cursed and stomped and raged, the puppet would not dance.

That evening, when Grandfather came home for his supper, Simon made sure he treated Lorette with tender care. He set her gently on the bench beside him while he ate and cradled her softly in his arms while he listened to Grandfather's stories beneath the night sky. Before he fell asleep on his straw mat in the corner of the hearth room, he carefully arranged her above his head so she wouldn't get crushed. And, all evening long, Grandfather studied every move he made with the precious marionette.

The next day Simon took Lorette to the far corner of the meadow to practice. He raised the left hand string. Lorette raised her arm. He raised the right hand string. Lorette raised her other arm. As slowly and patiently as he could, Simon tried to make the puppet dance. And though she turned a little smoother than the day before, she did not really dance.

"You're not a puppet," Simon yelled at her. "You're an ugly, clumsy thing!" Simon bundled up the strings and tossed Lorette as far as he could. She landed in the mud beside the stream. Simon left her there and climbed a tree, spending the rest of the morning shredding leaf after leaf, furiously.

Finally, when it was time to go for his noontime meal, he remembered Lorette. He climbed down the tree and ran to the creek to collect her. However, the puppet wasn't there. He searched the stream bank frantically, but he couldn't find her. All he could find were tiny pointed footprints heading down to the stream.

Simon shook his head as he stared at the footprints. He looked all around for signs of whoever had stolen the puppet away. There were none. No human footprints, except his own, decorated the soft mud. There were no signs of an animal either. Only the tiny footprints led across the bank to the stream.

"It must have been a bird of some sort, which has flown away. Or perhaps those are the tracks of a frog or salamander," Simon mused, but he knew those tracks weren't made by any living creature. Cautiously he crept down to the stream to look. The gleam of a silver slipper caught his eye.

Simon reached swiftly beneath the water and retrieved the marionette. As he pulled her out from the current, she sputtered and gasped for breath. Simon stared at her in disbelief as her body heaved and shook, then he screamed and dropped her back into the creek again.

Frozen by shock, Simon watched her swirl in an eddy around and around. She splashed awkwardly for shore, but was tangled in her strings. The weight of her wooden crossbar slowly dragged her down. Finally she cried out for help and Simon roused from his trance and rescued her again.

This time, as Simon held her in his hands, he was flooded with wonder. She coughed and sputtered and collapsed against his palms. Then, to his great disappointment, she turned stiff and wooden again.

With reverence, Simon laid her gently in the sunshine to dry. He untangled her strings and stretched them out flat, then smoothed her hair and her dress. One silver shoe had slipped from her toes and was dangling by the gleaming ribbon that bound it to her feet. Carefully, he pushed it back on and retied the bow.

From that day on, Simon didn't need to have his grandfather nearby in order for him to treat Lorette with care. He carried her lovingly wherever he went, and when he tried to work her strings, he did so tenderly. Still she wouldn't move gracefully. Still she stayed wooden and stiff. Simon didn't blame her. He had mistreated her terribly.

But every night, in his dreams, he saw the marionette dance.

After several days, Simon gave up trying to make Lorette dance. Instead he would take her for long walks in the forest and climb trees so they could sit together and listen to the birds sing. He built her a little bed of sticks for her to sleep on at night. Whatever he ate, he offered her a piece. She never ate it, and the other children always laughed at him for doing it, but his grandfather would often come quietly to his side and lay a reassuring hand on his shoulder.

Often as they walked in the green meadows overflowing with wildflowers, Simon thought of how she danced in his dreams—him pulling each string, she responding with ease to his direction. Once or twice he even picked up the wooden crossbar and imagined how he would make her dance if he could. First a long pirouette. Then a lunge. Then a leap. Then a gentle arching backwards. He imagined every step, knowing it would be beautiful if only she would dance.

All summer long, Grandfather never asked about the puppet. Simon knew though that he was treating her as Grandfather would. Even if she never danced for him as she had for Grandfather, Simon believed that Grandfather would let him keep her. Then, on the last night before he was to leave for home, Grandfather asked him to make Lorette dance.

"I can't," Simon sputtered.

"Is that so?" Grandfather questioned him. "Haven't you been treating her well?"

"Yes," Simon stammered, "of course I have."

"Then she should dance for you," Grandfather said with conviction. "Haven't you been practicing?"

Simon looked at his feet. "No," he mumbled weakly.

"Why not?" Grandfather asked sternly. "Don't you want to be a puppeteer?"

"Oh, yes," Simon assured him.

"Then you must try to make her dance." Grandfather pointed to Lorette, indicating that Simon should begin.

So Simon picked up the strings and moved them slowly. Lorette raised an arm shakily. Simon helped her twirl on pointed toes. Lorette looked very unsteady. Simon worked the strings again and again, making Lorette glide and leap and pirouette. Finally Simon laid down the strings and shrugged. "She doesn't want to, Grandfather."

Grandfather looked at him sternly with a heavy gaze. "Tomorrow," he said slowly, "you will leave her here when you go."

Simon stared in disbelief. "No! I must keep her!" he shouted as he clutched Lorette to him.

"I'm sorry, Simon," Grandfather said. "I cannot send her home with you."

"You must! You must!" Simon pleaded as his grandfather shook his head.

Then, unable to bear the thought of leaving without Lorette, Simon jumped up, turning for the door.

"It's no use," Grandfather called out to him. "If she won't dance, she doesn't want to be with you."

Simon didn't listen. He ran from the room and out into

the night, holding his beloved marionette tight to him. He ran across the meadows and into the trees, wanting to never return. He ran until he wasn't sure which way to turn anymore. He was only sure that he was far enough from Grandfather to be able to stop and rest.

Simon climbed a tree and sat, staring at Lorette. He remembered how beautiful she looked when he had rescued her from the stream. "Do you really hate me," he asked, "for throwing you in the mud that day?"

The puppet stared back with cold, painted eyes.

"I'm sorry," Simon said. "I had hoped you would forgive me, someday, and then you'd dance."

The puppet still lay lifeless in his hands. "At least," he said softly, "you dance in my dreams." Then Simon closed his eyes, wanting to sleep.

However, the moon shone bright in his face so, after a minute, Simon opened his eyes again. Then he realized his hands felt empty. He looked down for Lorette. She was gone.

Simon began to cry out, but then he saw her, sitting farther out along the branch of the tree. He caught his cry and silenced it. Then quietly he watched Lorette.

She was staring out at the moon. Her strings were wound neatly around the wooden bar and held in her hands. The silver of her slippers gleamed in the moonshine and her face was radiant with light.

"I forgave you long ago for that day by the stream," she said sadly.

"Then why?" Simon wondered, trembling with the excitement of speaking with her. "Why would you not dance?"

"You never asked," she answered simply. "You never really spoke to me as if I could answer."

"I did," Simon said slowly. "Didn't I?"

"Not out loud. Not with your whole heart. Not as if I were real," Lorette replied. "You were still the puppeteer and I the puppet."

"But I thought I was being good to you, not to ask. I thought, if you didn't want to dance, I shouldn't make you," Simon offered.

"I'm a ballerina. I love to dance." Lorette turned to look at him. There were tears in her eyes. She stood up and walked the branch back to him. She stared at him with deep brown eyes. "But when I dance, you cannot be in charge. You cannot be the master."

"But I want to be your puppeteer. I want to take care of you. I want to help you dance!" Simon protested.

"If I were just a wooden doll, you could treat me so," Lorette explained. "But even though you've learned to treat me gently, you must still learn I am not like any other marionette."

"What must I do?" Simon asked softly.

"Set me free, in your heart, to dance."

"How?" Simon whispered hopefully.

"Raise my strings, but do not control them in any way. Only keep them from getting tangled."

So there in the moonlight, Simon raised the crossbar high and Lorette danced along the tree branch. She was even more graceful than Simon remembered from the first time he had seen her dance. He found he really had little to do with her movements, for Lorette turned whichever way she pleased. He only had to be there with her and hold the strings gently in his hands.

"Why don't I just cut you free of the strings?" Simon asked when she was through. "You don't need them or me, either."

Then she smiled at him and sighed. "But I do. We are a team. I need you there to hold these strings which steady me."

Simon held out the palm of his hands for Lorette to step onto. "I'm glad." He grinned back. "Otherwise, I would be useless."

"No need for that," Lorette assured him. "I'll dance for you when you ask as I danced for your grandfather."

Then, as Simon climbed down the tree and headed back through the woods, he realized how different he was from the boy who had first tried to make Lorette dance. His need to be in charge had stopped her from dancing as it had stopped him from getting along with anyone. Now, things would be different.

Then, as they crossed the stream near his grandfather's meadow, he remembered a question he had long wanted to ask her. "Why did you fall into the creek that day?"

"I was washing the mud from my dress," Lorette explained, "and my strings fell into the current and pulled me down."

Simon shook his head at himself. "I used to be so stupid," he said with a sigh.

Lorette looked up at him and touched him tenderly. "No," she replied. "You just believed, like many believe, that you could be this puppet's master."

LOVING VOICES

Once upon a time, in the darkness of a cold winter night, a young boy named Luke lay very still, straining to hear beyond the stone walls of the little hut where he lived. He lay beneath his blanket of fur, barely breathing, afraid he would miss that wonderfully deep voice of the owl which he listened for. Somewhere, Luke knew, an owl was peering through the night with large yellow eyes, ready to break the silence of the great forest with its echoing call. Tonight, Luke wanted to keep awake to hear that owl.

Luke waited and waited, hearing only silence, until someone in the one-room hut coughed and turned over in their sleep. It was Sarah, his younger sister, and the noise she made, as she rustled beneath her sleeping furs, interfered with his listening.

Taking a deep breath of the frosty air within the room, Luke sighed with anger and frustration. Sarah had been so cruel all day, with a voice like iron. She had been delighted at the pain in his eyes when she squashed a spider he was watching. She had laughed out loud as he whistled to the deer herd in the meadow. Then she yelled to scare them all away. Now, Sarah was restless in her sleep, making it difficult to listen for the owl when he wanted so much to hear it.

Luke couldn't remember a night, since the first winter snow, when he hadn't listened for the owl. There was something in him that needed to hear it—to ease the pain he felt in his heart and to ready him for another day with Sarah and Mother and Father. When the nights grew warmer he would have bullfrogs and crickets to cheer to him. In the winter, though, he only had the owls.

Sarah settled, at last, and Luke strained again to listen to the forest outside his home. For a long time there was nothing but the crack of the cold tree limbs. Then, he felt it. He always felt it first. It was a pang that shot through his heart, filling him with longing till the first notes came. Finally, muffled by the distance through the trees, each note sang out, probing the night till it reached him in the darkness.

"Hoo, hoohoo, hoo, hoo."

Luke held his breath, expectant. There was a pause and then a higher-pitched reply. "Hoo, hoohoo, hoo, hoo."

Luke smiled. It was his first smile that day. Then he closed his eyes peacefully and fell asleep.

Morning shattered that peace with the sharp call of his mother. "Luke," she screeched. "Luke. Get up."

A foot poked him in the side as his mother's bony figure leaned over him. "Luke. You're always the last to wake up."

"Yes, Mother," Luke mumbled. "I was dreaming."

"No time for dreams," Luke's father muttered sternly from the table in the center of the room. "Don't waste your time on them. There's chores and chores and chores."

"He's always dreaming," Sarah grumbled from the other side of the table, "or watching bugs and things, or staring at the sky, or whistling to deer, or talking to rabbits, or counting flower petals. He never listens to anyone. Never at all."

Luke tuned out Sarah's grumbling and his mother's screeching. He looked away from his father, sitting silent and stern, and pulled on his clothes. After rolling up his sleeping furs, he sat down to eat, as sullen as his father.

All that morning Luke worked hard cutting wood, repairing the wagon and sharpening tools. Like always, he did everything his father needed except tend the traps. Luke's father had learned years ago not to send Luke out to the traps. Luke couldn't stand to see the animals in pain—their leg caught in the trap's sharp teeth—so he would always come back empty handed, saying nothing had been caught. Secretly, though, he had set the animals free and, if they were already dead, he had buried them quietly in the moist earth of the silent forest.

Luke's father went out to the traps each day, and brought home dead animals to skin so their pelts could be stretched out on frames. They made their living by trapping furs, and sometimes Luke's father needed help with the skins. Luke would do as he was told, to avoid a whipping, but he always wondered why people valued furs more than the creatures that once lived inside them. The furs were soft, but they were such dead things—empty and lifeless—like Sarah and Mother and Father.

That afternoon, when all the skins were mounted and the tools put away, Luke had time to walk alone in the woods. He slipped behind the tool shed and onto a path that led through the meadow. Sarah was there, fetching water from the brook. Luke walked right past her, without a word. Then Sarah turned and called to him as he walked away through the trees, "Go... go on... I hope you never come back."

Luke turned to look at her from the shadow of an oak. She was getting tall and stiff and bony like their mother. What had happened to her? What had made her become like them? Her voice was as hard and dead as a stone. She glared at him, like Mother glared at Father. And just like Father, he turned and walked away.

It wasn't the first time that it dawned on him. He had known for a while that he was becoming like Father—distant and withdrawn and sober. Maybe that's why he turned more and more to the forest for comfort, searching for some clue in the dark woods that would lead him beyond that dreary life his father lived.

And perhaps, now, that was why he kept on walking deeper and deeper into the forest, making his way along overgrown paths that disappeared and reappeared and then faded away altogether. At first he wasn't aware that he was crying, but as he brushed away the remnant of a spider web from his cheek, he found his hand was wet.

Then the silent tears became a trembling sob. He stumbled on every rock or stick or root that filled his path. Yet he kept walking, deeper and deeper into the woods—away from his family. Twilight filled the spaces around him, quickly, so he didn't notice. And each time he fell down, he rose and moved on, but as he did the pain inside his heart grew until he couldn't walk any more.

He stopped beside an outcrop of stone and leaned against it. The trembling in him grew. He stared at the sky between the branches of a tree. Finally, the trembling swelled inside his throat and a wail broke from it as loud and forlorn as a wolf's midnight cry. It felt like some ancient instinct in him had finally been set free, and Luke let it flow for a long, long time.

Deep inside, Luke knew he was calling. Who he was calling or what he was calling he didn't know, but he called with all his might. Then Luke paused. He stood expectant, the air ringing with the longing he felt. Finally that familiar pang hit him in his heart, telling him the owl was near.

"Hoo, hoohoo, hoo, hoo."

Luke held his breath and waited. Then came the higher-pitched reply. "Hoo, hoohoo, hoo, hoo."

Luke smiled and relaxed into the rock, savoring each note, locking it into his memory. He felt himself sigh with relief. Then he heard the whisper of wings.

"Hoo, hoohoo, hoo, hoo."

Luke looked up startled. Three? He had never heard three owls. Bewildered, Luke glanced around him. There was another whisper on the air and then a shadow crossed the gloom of twilight in the forest. All at once, Luke realized how late it had become. It was nightfall, and the trees around him were alive with large yellow eyes.

"Hoo, hoohoo, hoo, hoo."
"Hoo, hoohoo, hoo, hoo."

Now Luke could see their shadows, perhaps twenty or thirty of them in the branches of the trees. They formed a circle around him. Most were large with tiny tufts, like pointed ears, on top of their heads. A few were small and slender. All were watching him. He felt overcome with awe. He knew somehow he had called them, and they had come.

Luke stood silent, waiting to see what the owls would do. Then, to his surprise, one owl called, "Hoo, hoohoo, whoo? Who is it?"

Luke looked up into a pair of bright eyes. They blinked at him as the owl answered the question himself. "Ah, yes. I know who. It is Luke."

"Luke. Luke," a second owl called.

"Luke. Hello, Luke," hooted another.

Luke sank to the ground dumfounded. He shook his head, trying to rid himself of the eerie feeling that the owls could speak. But, still, they called to him.

"Luke."

"Luke."

"Luke."

Again and again, the owls voices flooded him, washing him with comfort. Finally Luke stopped fighting it. It might be a dream, he thought, but he didn't care. He could be crazy, but if he was he didn't care. There was something in the owls' voices that he hadn't heard in years—something soft, something warm, something loving.

"Luke."

"Luke."

Luke looked around him, watching those yellow eyes. The owls continued to call his name. Each voice had a different quality, but all were loving. Each owl spoke his name at least a hundred times. And every time he heard their loving voice he felt his pain disappear.

At last the owls fell silent. Luke looked upward toward their shadows in the trees. There was nothing he needed and there was nothing he needed to say. He knew they understood his gratitude. One by one, he faced them. And one by one, they rose in silence and flew away.

Finally he was alone. He curled against the rocky outcrop and covered himself with a bank of dry leaves from the forest floor to keep warm. Then, with a glowing smile and a warm heart, he slept.

However, morning brought a new kind of pain. He woke hungry. He'd missed his supper and the cold of the night had burnt whatever energy he'd had in reserve. Now his stomach ached from its emptiness. He would have to go home.

He looked around him and realized he didn't know which way was home. When he left his sister yesterday, he had headed west. Yet, in his journey, he could have turned any direction. Luke looked for the sun. In the morning it was in the east. Perhaps that was the way he should go.

And then he thought of home. He didn't know if he wanted to return, even though his hunger drove him to it. He thought of Sarah and Mother and Father with their hard, cruel voices, so unlike the loving voices he'd heard last night. No, he didn't want to go home. He wanted to grow wings and fly with the owls.

Luke slumped beneath a tree. He felt the pain gnawing at his stomach and in his heart he felt his old pain return. He would have to choose between the two and he wasn't sure the pain of hunger would win. Then he realized he was holding something.

Luke opened his palm to find a small oblong pellet in his hand. It was gray and soft. When he broke it open there were tiny little bones inside. Luke knew it was the fur and bones that an owl had spat out after eating its prey. Looking into the tree above him for the owl, he saw something that made him jump.

There, on one of the branches, was a tiny man about as large as a great horned owl. He wore a cloak of feathers that opened out like wings. His hair peaked on each side of his head like the tufts of an owl and his eyes were large and round and yellow.

Luke stammered as he stared at the little man, "I... I thought you were an owl."

"I am," the man hooted. "I am."

Luke shook his head. "But you look like a man."

"I do," the man said with a nod.

"But how?"

"We can change our form, sometimes, when we need to speak with... with different words."

"Like last night?" Luke wondered.

"Yes," the little owl-man grinned, "and today."

Luke put his hand against the tree and smiled. He recognized the voice. This had been the first owl, last night, to speak—the one who knew his name. "But how did you know my name?" he asked, bewildered.

"Because I've seen you many times in these woods. I've watched you grow. I've felt you awake in the night, listening for my call. How could I not know your name?"

Luke looked up at the owl-man, filled with awe. "And you followed me yesterday? You followed me here?"

The little man hooted and shook his head. "No, I didn't have to follow you. You walked in circles all that time. This is my tree. You came to my tree."

Suddenly a panic shot through Luke. He stared at the owl-man, then looked through the trees.

"Yes," the owl-man answered. "Your home is over there. It is a ways, but not that far." The little man fluttered his cape. "You are not lost."

Luke slumped against the tree in despair. The pain swelled inside him. Then he looked hopefully at the little man. "I don't want to go home. I want to be an owl-man like you."

The little man fluttered his cape again, but this time he

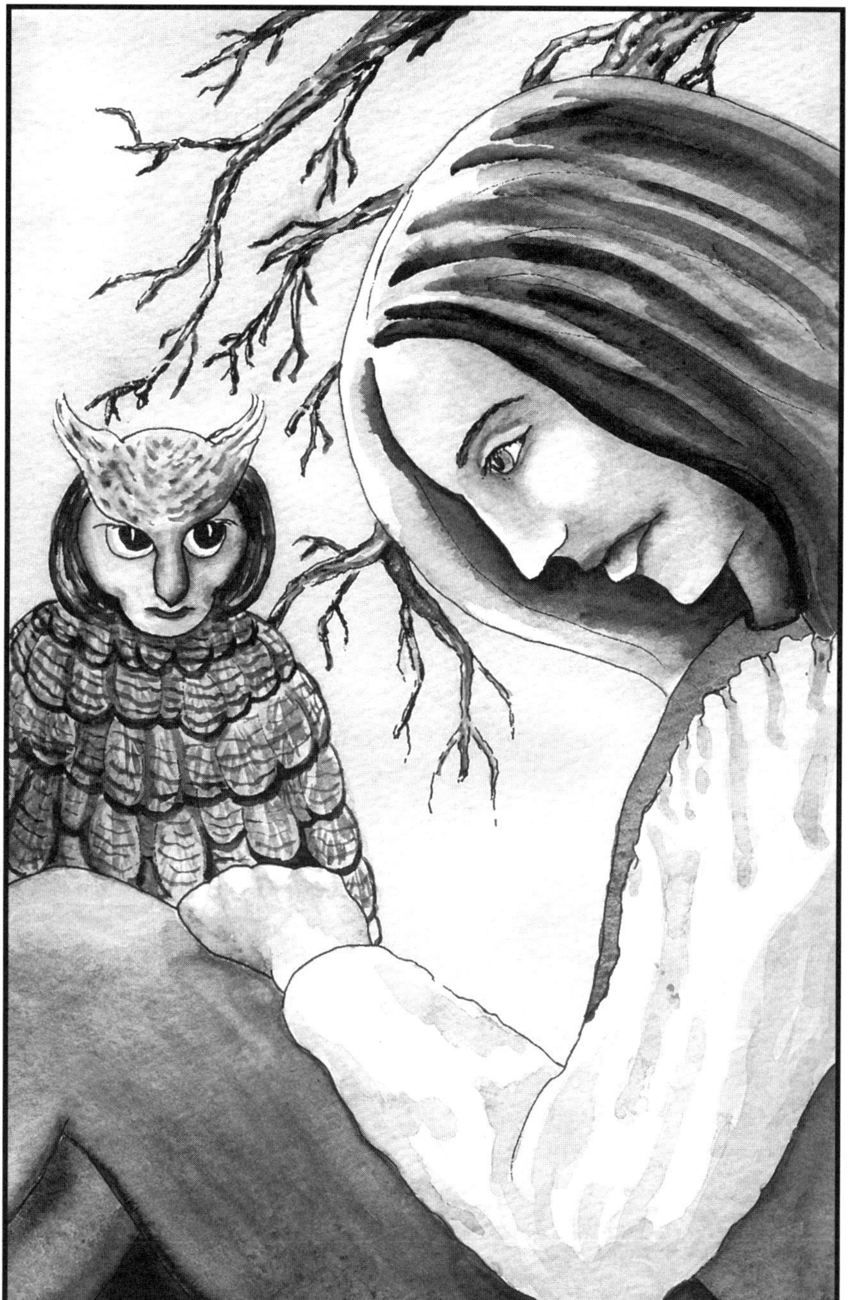

left the branch and glided to the ground. He stood, blinking at Luke indignantly. "I am not a man. I am an owl. You are not an owl. You are a boy."

"But it hurts so much to be a boy. People are cold and dead. Their voices are like ice, without love." He leaned close to the little man. "I want to hear the loving voices like I heard last night."

The man looked at him for a long time, his yellow eyes unblinking. Luke hoped he was considering some magical way to transform a human into an owl. It was a shock to Luke when the owl-man said, "Then you must be the loving voice."

Luke sat back in alarm. He shuddered. Something in him understood. He didn't answer though. He just stared at those bright yellow eyes.

"You must be the loving voice," the owl-man repeated. "It is that simple. You will find more loving voices when you become one."

Luke's thoughts went immediately to his sister, Sarah. He imagined, for a moment, speaking to her in a loving way. Then his mind clamped shut. No. Not her, or Mother or Father.

Suddenly the little man turned his head, in owl-like fashion, to look directly behind him through the trees. There was a crack of a branch and a cough. Instantly, the cape fluttered in front of Luke. Then the little man was rising into the tree on silent wings, fully feathered—an owl again.

Luke heard a second cough. He shrank back into the shadow of the tree. In the distance, he saw his sister, walking aimlessly. Her shoulders were sunken. Her head hung limp. She walked closer and closer.

All at once there was a rustle in the branches above him.

"Hoo, hoohoo, hoo, hoo," the owl called.

Luke jumped in alarm. His sister looked straight at him. He stared back at her. They stood there, watching each other for what seemed like eternity. And in that long, long moment, Luke dared to remember her as she was years ago—full of laughter and fun and mischief. He wondered, would it ever be possible for her to be that way again?

Then he thought of the owl's words: *Be the loving voice.* Something in him stirred. It was like the whisper of wings in his heart.

"Sarah," he said and then he repeated it, letting the sound open up to carry the feeling he felt. "Sarah."

Sarah stood frozen on the spot, but he could see his voice had touched her. Her mouth dropped open.

"Sarah," Luke repeated, letting the word ring with feeling.

Suddenly, Sarah burst into tears. She shook her head and stomped her foot in anger. "Why?" she sobbed. "Why haven't you said it for so long? My name. You haven't said it for years."

"Sarah," Luke said, "I know and I'm sorry."

"You've been just like Father," Sarah continued, "so silent and mean. You would never even say my name."

Luke stepped forward. He took his sister's hand and squeezed it gently. "I will never be like Father again. I promise, Sarah. I promise."

Sarah grew silent, her eyes overflowing. He looked at them and saw what she had held inside for so long. It was a pain like his. It was the very same pain.

"Last night," Sarah said, her voice trembling with sorrow, "I heard a call—it was wild and fierce and I thought it was you and you were dying and I felt dead too. I've been walking all night to find you."

This time Luke didn't say anything. Tears broke through the silence. He was crying and she was crying. Then they were laughing both together. It was a wild, free laugh from deep within the pain and the tears. For a long time, that laughter filled the forest.

Finally Sarah grabbed her brother's arm. "Luke," she said. "Oh, Luke. What will we do about Mother and Father? We'll be so different. Will they understand?"

"I don't know," said Luke. "But it doesn't matter."

Then as if to acknowledge what he said, Luke heard a rustle in the branches above. He looked at the owl's tree and smiled. "Listen," he said to Sarah. "Listen."

Then, together, they heard the owl's loving voice, "Hoo, hoohoo, hoo, hoo."

And in the distance a higher voice answered, "Hoo, hoohoo, hoo, hoo."

THE EARTH WITCH

A long time ago, there was an island kingdom whose mountains rose high above the sea. The mountains were green, rugged and rich with beauty. They towered over the great port cities which hugged the coastline of the huge island. However, though many lived in the cities or in the surrounding countryside, no one dared to live in the mountains—not only because they were steep and heavily forested, but because they belonged to the Earth Witch.

Some people still came to the mountains, though, to hike the forest trails. One, a girl named Rayna, came in her family's buggy every week. She'd make the driver wait for hours while she hiked through towering trees and quiet meadows. She hardly met anyone, as she walked, for the mountains were vast and the visitors few. Often she imagined, as she looked from the ridge tops, that everything she saw was hers.

In fact, there were many times she begged her father to

buy the mountains, since he was a very wealthy man. "Buy the mountains?" he would say with a laugh. "I cannot buy the mountains. No one ever will."

"But I must have them," Rayna would plead. "I must have them, please."

"There is no way." He would shake his head. "The Earth Witch watches the mountains. She always guards them. There is no one that can take them away."

And though she inquired of everyone how she might buy the mountains, they always told her it was impossible. The Earth Witch, who cast a spell on any who harmed even a single tree, would not let her. So, one day, Rayna gave up the idea of buying the mountains and, instead, set her heart on stealing them from the Earth Witch.

That day Rayna didn't hike her favorite trails. Instead she sat at the top of a ridge, watching the forest below her for a sign of the Earth Witch. In Rayna's mind, the Earth Witch was a crazy old woman who spread rumors about herself and used a few tricks to keep people away. Rayna was sure, if she could just track down the old woman, she could take the mountains from her without a fuss.

She walked the ridge all afternoon, hoping to see someone in the valleys around her. Then, as she sat on a rock staring at a fog bank on the sea, someone tapped her on the shoulder. "Hello," said a girl's pleasant voice.

Rayna turned to see a girl, perhaps a year older than her, standing beside the rock. Her clothes were clean but rather worn and strangely old-fashioned.

"I saw you from the other ridge," the girl explained. "You've been up here all day."

Rayna looked at her suspiciously. "I didn't see you."

The girl laughed and pointed to a brown cloak draped

over her arm. "I blend with the shadows," she explained. Then she turned to survey the view. "Isn't this the most beautiful place in the world?"

"Yes, it is." Rayna sighed. "I wish it were mine."

"What on earth for?" asked the girl.

"Just because I love it so." Rayna sighed again. She stared, for a short time, at the craggy peaks that rose above her. Then, when she turned back to the girl, she found herself alone.

"How rude!" Rayna said with a huff. She looked for a trace of a brown-cloaked figure slipping through the shadows. However there was none, only the sound of a soft hum. It made Rayna shiver and suddenly she realized the Earth Witch might not be a crazy old woman as she had imagined.

After that day, Rayna spent more and more time in the mountains looking for a sign of the Earth Witch or the girl, wondering if they were the same. There were times when she felt someone watching her, but she saw only shadows in the forest. And there were times when she heard that strange hum, almost like the wind in the trees, but she could never find out what it was. At last she decided to trick the witch with a careful plan she had devised.

It was early one morning when Rayna came to the mountains with an axe. She climbed to the top of that same rocky ridge where she had spoken with the girl. Satisfied that she was in clear view of anyone close by, she took the axe and struck a lonesome looking, twisted pine which clung to the granite on the ridge top.

Rayna listened carefully. She heard the wind spring up. The tree groaned as it bent with the gusts. Clouds seemed to darken above her. She struck again and again. The wind came roaring down on her, but she also heard that other sound beyond the roar. It was a low hum that grew louder with each mark she made into the tree's bark. Then satisfied she had done enough, she laid down the axe and hid behind a boulder.

The storm hovered above her as if deciding whether to break into a full force gale. She felt very cold, with the wind whipping around her, but she pulled her cloak tight and waited. Gradually the humming sound grew, and when it was loud enough to be very close, she peeked around the boulder carefully. She smiled at what she saw.

Before the tree stood the girl, dressed in the brown cloak. She was holding something in her hand that looked like a round stone. Rayna realized that the girl was singing very softly. She couldn't hear the words, but it was a gentle song like a mother's lullaby. The song went on for several minutes. Finally it stopped. Then the girl stood very still, holding the stone out toward the tree.

All at once, as Rayna watched, the wounds she had made in the tree began to heal. Slowly, one at a time, they disappeared as the girl touched the stone to the bark. Finally, when the tree was completely free of any scar, the witch girl turned the stone and her song toward the axe.

It was then, without thinking, that Rayna dashed out to grab the stone. She was suddenly obsessed with the small rock. She had planned to watch the witch for many days, learning her ways, looking for her weaknesses. But now the stone called out to her. She couldn't resist.

In a second, she had her hands around the stone, yanking it from the other girl. Rayna stared at it for a brief moment, cradled in her palms. Then, with a scream, she dropped the stone as a terrible pain shot through her arms. The pain raced through her chest into the very core of her.

She fainted.

When Rayna awoke, the sky was darkening but the wind was calm. Rayna glanced toward the scraggly pine. There wasn't a sign of the wounds she had made. The axe lay beside her. Its edge looked melted, making it too blunt to ever harm another tree. Rayna picked it up and searched for the Earth Witch. She listened for her hum. Both were gone, so she hurried down the hill to go home. Yet, as she left in her buggy, she felt very uneasy as if the trees were watching her leave.

Her uneasiness faded quickly, however, for her ambition to own the mountains was very strong. Rayna returned the next day, not with an axe, but with a brown cloak like the witch girl's. All day long she practiced slipping from shadow to shadow, blending in with the trees. Finally, near noontime, she walked to the top of the ridge and waited. At last she heard that low hum of the Earth Witch.

Carefully, she crept to the edge of a meadow, where the Earth Witch knelt beside a fawn. The little creature looked dazed, and Rayna could see an arrow in its right hind leg. The witch girl took the stone from a pouch around her neck and held it close to the fawn as she sang softly. Slowly, the arrow crumbled into dust and the wound healed. Then, wobbling to its feet, the little fawn gently licked the witch's hand.

A jab of envy shot into Rayna's heart. The Earth Witch not only owned the mountains—even timid creatures, like the fawn, were her friends. Rayna felt in her pocket for the heavy gloves she had brought. With them, she would take the stone from the Earth Witch for that seemed to be the source of her magic.

And though she put the gloves on, she didn't race out to snatch the stone away. Instead, she followed the girl for most of the afternoon. She watched with curiosity as the witch girl stopped to heal the stem of a moonflower, toppled by a footstep, or a limb broken by a human's fall. However, there were many broken limbs and flower stems and even an injured bird which the Earth Witch didn't mend. Rayna sensed these were acts of nature, and the witch girl let nature's ways alone.

Finally, in the late afternoon, Rayna saw the witch enter a small cottage nestled in a thick grove of trees. The roof was mossy and the walls made from a black stone. It was very, very hard to see the cottage in the darkness of the shadows, and as Rayna peeked into a window, she felt as if she was the first human to ever peer inside.

The cottage was furnished very simply. In the corner, there was a bed of woven twigs, shaped round like a nest and filled with moss. Near the door, was a gnarled stump that probably served as a stool and a stone table which held a cup and a bucket. The Earth Witch turned to that now and dipped the cup into the bucket. She took a long drink, then took off the pouch that held the stone and laid it on the table. At last, she lay peacefully on the bed as if asleep.

Rayna waited for a long time. The Earth Witch didn't stir. Finally she crept to the door and opened it slowly. It gave an eerie creak. Rayna's heart raced as she stared at the witch girl. However the noise didn't penetrate the witch's sleep. The girl still lay motionless.

Sneaking across the room on tiptoe, Rayna grabbed the pouch in her gloved hands. She stared at it for a moment, feeling triumph in her heart. Then she looked toward the Earth Witch. The girl was sitting up, wide awake.

For a moment, they stood face to face. Rayna felt the stone throbbing in her gloved hands, but the pain was very

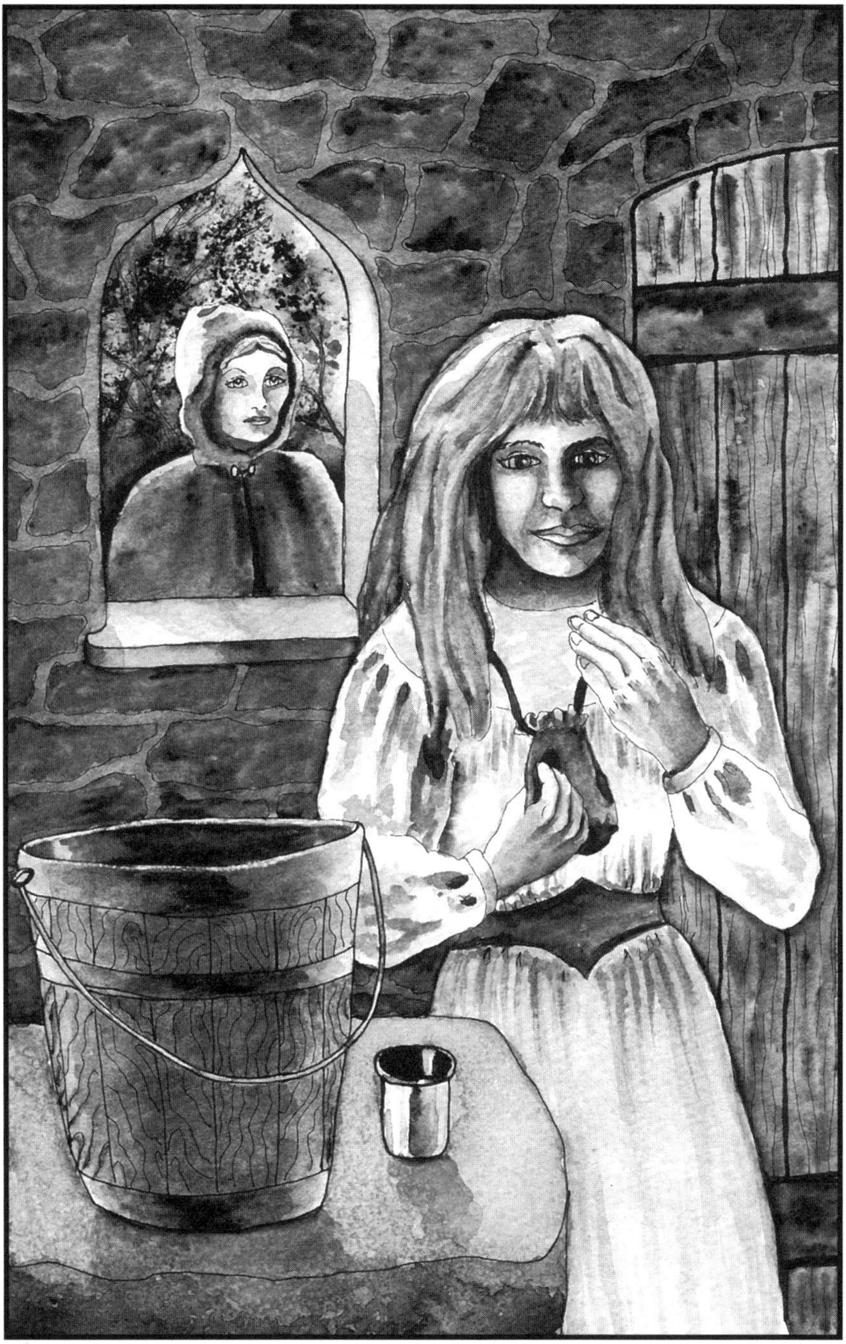

faint. She tightened her grip on the pouch and called out, "I'm hiding this so you will never find it. And without it, you can not own the mountains. Now I do."

Then Rayna raced through the door and down the mountains toward the buggy which waited far below. As she ran, she heard the witch girl calling to her. She didn't stop. She kept on running, feeling wildly giddy with her victory.

It was only as the buggy clattered down the road toward the city, that Rayna looked back. There was the Earth Witch at the end of the trail, not yelling in anger, but smiling and waving. Rayna felt a moment of confusion, then decided it was one last trick by the Earth Witch to make the stone appear unimportant. She clutched it tighter and hardly noticed how the muffled throbbing grew fainter and fainter with each turn of the carriage wheel.

For the first few weeks after she defeated the Earth Witch, Rayna walked among the trees joyfully, elated with her triumph. She found the witch's cottage again, after many days of wandering. It was deserted. She saw no sign of the witch girl anywhere among the trees. She heard no soft hum.

Jubilantly, Rayna realized the girl had left the forest, now that the stone and her power were gone. Yet, somewhere deep within, Rayna felt disturbed. She held that image in her mind of the witch girl, smiling and waving as the buggy raced away. It haunted her and she didn't know why.

Soon enough, though, Rayna realized her victory was not complete. One day, when she came to the mountains, she passed a team of horses, pulling a wagon load of logs. Another day, she saw a hunter with five deer carcasses piled high on a mule. Within a week, she found a tall, burly man, building a crude log cabin in a meadow.

She raced up to the him and shouted, "You can't do this!

These are my mountains!"

He just laughed at her. "These mountains belong to no one. This land is all free."

That night she complained to her father. "He's right." Her father sighed. "The mountains are public with no laws to protect them. There has always been the Earth Witch to guard them. I wonder where she's gone?"

Rayna grew silent for a moment. Then she brightened. "We could pass laws."

"True," said her father, "if everyone can agree. However it could take years."

Rayna burst into tears. "But by that time, the mountains will be destroyed!"

She ran to the garden where the pouch was hidden and grabbed the stone. And, though it was late, she badgered the driver to take her back to the mountains. There, she ran up to the meadow where the newly built walls of the cabin stood. But, though she hummed and sang and held the stone high, nothing happened to the logs of the cabin or the tree stumps that had been cut to make it. Defeated, she returned to the buggy and went home.

After a few months, Rayna didn't even go to the mountains anymore. It broke her heart to see more trees being cut, more creatures killed, more houses built and farmland cleared. She walked the streets of her city, instead, searching for the Earth Witch.

It took six months to find her. The girl had aged years in that time. She now looked like the old woman Rayna had first imagined. She still wore the same old-fashioned clothes and brown cloak as she had in the mountains. Now they looked tattered and torn.

Rayna watched quietly from an alley as the old woman

stepped up to a child crying in the street. The boy had fallen and scraped his knee. The woman helped him up and spoke to him quietly. Then with a pass of her hand and a little hum, the scrape was gone.

"There, run along now," Rayna heard the woman say before continuing up the cobbled street. Slowly the woman made her way toward the bay, picking up litter and smiling at everyone who came along.

Rayna followed her to a tiny driftwood shack hidden beneath a bridge that crossed the bay. Just as the woman entered the door, she turned to look at Rayna. "Come in," she invited with a pleasant smile.

Rayna nodded and stepped inside the shack. The woman motioned to her to sit down on a gnarled stump, worn smooth by the sea. Rayna shook her head and turned to face her, holding the pouch with the stone out toward the woman. "I've come to give you back the stone."

The woman smiled. "It's not my stone anymore."

"But the mountains need you. The trees, the deer, the flowers—everything is being destroyed."

"I am no longer the Earth Witch. I can't help you," the woman explained. "One can't be the Earth Witch forever. There is even more important work to do."

"But without an Earth Witch, the forest will be overrun by people," Rayna argued.

"Oh, there is an Earth Witch," the woman assured her.

"Where is she? Please tell me," Rayna pleaded.

The woman looked at her and chuckled. "You are the Earth Witch, my girl. You accepted the task when you took the stone."

"No!" Rayna shook her head. "Not me. I can't live in that cottage in the trees. My father would never let me."

The old woman nodded. "Yes, I had a family too. But sometimes people get lost in the wilderness and are never found."

"What would I eat?" Rayna demanded.

The woman shrugged. "I never felt hungry. I just drank from the bucket. It was all I ever needed."

Rayna looked at the woman confused. Then she remembered the stone in her hand. Her voice trembled as she protested one last time, "I can't be the Earth Witch. The stone won't work for me."

The old woman touched her shoulder gently. "You will succeed when you can feel the pain of the injured things—of the trees and the plants and the creatures—and feel it without fear."

Rayna shuddered, thinking of the pain she felt when she first touched the stone. "It's too much. The pain is so strong. I can't do it."

"You can," the old woman explained, "if you invoke the love."

The old woman sat down on the twisted stump. She motioned for Rayna to sit on the floor beside her. Rayna looked up into that wrinkled face and kind smile. "How?" she asked quietly.

"Everything—the trees, the deer, the flowers, the stones—are expressions of love. Their nature is love, nothing more. When humans misuse the forest, they try to impose something other than love on its magnificence. To heal the forest, you must call to that love."

"But the pain?" Rayna questioned.

"You will feel the pain till you are certain only love is there."

Rayna sat for a long time, staring at the stone in her

hands. "Is there magic in the stone to help me?"

The old woman rose and motioned her toward the door. Then she took off her ragged brown cloak and wrapped it around the girl. "The only magic in anything is the power of the love within it. If you lost this stone, any stone would do."

"And the song?" Rayna looked at her in awe.

"Any song."

Rayna stepped through the door as if the woman had mesmerized her with a spell. She walked along the marshy shore of the bay, feeling numb. She clutched the pouch in her hand and pulled the brown cloak around her. In a stupor, she walked the whole day.

It was way past sunset when Rayna found herself opening the door to the little cottage hidden in the grove of trees. She stepped inside and went to the stone table. Picking up the cup, she dipped it into the pail and drank. It was only water, but it nourished her like nothing had before. It tasted soothing, like a cup of joy.

And then she felt the throbbing of the stone. She put the pouch around her neck and took the stone from within it. The pain shot through her hands. She dropped it twice before she could even hold it. Finally, she began to hum.

The humming helped. It was as if the pain could dissipate through her voice into the air. She stepped beyond the cottage. The pain grew stronger. And, like the cry of a wounded creature, she followed the call of the pain as it grew.

Not far from the grove, she found a fox in a steel-jawed trap. The animal lay motionless as she bent toward it. She held the stone out to it and she stared at the ugly wound in the animal's leg. With all her might, she called through her song to the pain in the fox and strived to see the love that lay within. The creature stirred, but still there was no healing and the pain within the stone was very great.

For an instant, her voice wavered. Her head felt faint. And then it came to her to look at the teeth of the trap. At first she felt only hate for that jagged steel, but quickly she remembered the old woman's wisdom—everything was an expression of love, even the metal this trap was made of. She knew she must call on the love within it to heal the fox.

She stopped singing. The pain rose in intensity. She felt its full force. Then she stared at the trap. She thought of all the harm it had done. And then she said to it, with a knowing that was sure, "You are love, only love. And as love you cannot harm. The shape the humans gave you is no more."

Suddenly the pain was transformed into a different feeling. It was intense, but it hurt her no more. The steel teeth melted before her eyes, releasing their hold on the fox. Instantly, the leg healed.

And then Rayna's eyes met those of the fox. In them, she saw only love. She held out her hand. The fox licked it in gratitude. She watched him stand and run deep into the forest shadows.

Finally, she stood up, went into the cottage and quietly closed the door.

STEPPING THROUGH:
MOMENTS OF TRANSFORMATION

WAITING FOR DRAGON

Once there was a girl who was tall and thin and rather quiet. She lived in a cottage at the edge of the village next to her father's blacksmith shop. She was neither rich nor poor, smart nor foolish, beautiful nor ugly. Except for her unusual height, she was a very average girl, and she felt her life was boring.

Her name was Beth and every day she woke to the sharp words of her mother calling her to the kitchen to fix breakfast. She would rise and dress herself slowly. Then she would go downstairs, reluctantly, one step at a time. She always paused before opening the kitchen door. Then she would step inside, knowing how this day would start and how this day would end. Beth wanted, more than anything, for her life to change, yet she couldn't imagine how it would happen.

Very early one winter morning Beth woke to a voice much different than her mother's. It was dark. There was something scratching at the shutters on her window. The voice whispered hoarsely, hissing slightly as it spoke her name, "Bethsss... Bethsss..."

Beth pulled her heavy quilt over her head so she couldn't hear it. The scratching grew louder. The shutters wobbled against the hinge with a soft creak, creak. She told herself it was just the wind. Perhaps the winter storms were coming at last. Her father had mentioned how late they were this year.

Still, as she tried to dismiss the words in the darkness, excitement trembled within her. Beth knew that this was different. This was new. This day would not be the same as all the others. How could she choose to hide in bed and miss it. How could she not greet the hissing voice?

Twice Beth tried to open the shutters. Each time she found herself halfway there, frozen to the floor, unable to go any further. Both times she raced back to the safety of her quilt and stayed hidden for what seemed like forever. Yet, the voice continued to call her name.

Finally she asked, "What do you want?"

"Bethsss," the hoarse voice answered, "I have a message from Dragon."

"D-dd-dragon?" Beth shivered as she stuttered the name. "I don't know any dragon."

"Dragon knowsss you," the voice replied. "I will ssslip the message between the ssshutters. Read it."

Beth stared across the room. She could hear a rustling noise in the darkness. Something dropped to the floor. She rose, and raced to the shutters. Opening them with trembling hands, she gazed into the shadows of the predawn twilight. Nothing was there.

Then she heard something scuttle across the roof slates. She saw a long, slim silhouette against the brightening sky. It looked like a large lizard, about the size of a broom. There were ridges of spines along its back. It turned to look at her before it slipped over the edge of the roof. It hissed, "Read it, Bethsss."

All at once it was gone. Beth studied the shadows on all the rooftops and the cobbled lane below. There was no sign of the creature. Its hoarse voice had vanished, but its words remained: *Read it, Bethsss.*

She picked up a parchment from the floor. In the gathering grayness of the light she saw there were only three words to the message. She read the words out loud, "I am coming." She looked at them blankly and read it again, "I am coming." She stared at the signature. It was simply: *Dragon.*

Bewildered, yet in awe, Beth sat on her bed and read the message over and over. Questions poured into her mind. Who is Dragon—a person or beast, a he or she? When is it coming? What is it coming for? Is Dragon a friend? Is Dragon real? Is Dragon magic?

There were no answers to any of these questions, so she just stared at the thick, rough parchment. It was bare except for the black ink of the writing and a small seal below the name stamped in gold. The seal was of a dragon in silhouette, long and spiny like the lizard creature had been, but with giant outstretched wings. Beth gazed at the dragon for a long time.

Finally she rolled up the parchment and hid it in a corner of her room. Then she dressed and went downstairs to do her chores. Later, when her mother entered the kitchen, she was surprised to see Beth cooking breakfast.

"What's this? Already up?" her mother said approvingly. "This is a change."

Beth just smiled and thought of her secret. "Yes," she

agreed. "It is different."

A month went by quickly. Every morning Beth rose early and did her chores. Then she helped her father in the blacksmith shop or played with the other children in the lane. When the church bell rang, she ran to class to do her lessons. She felt eager to work, eager to play and eager to learn, knowing at any moment Dragon might appear. Life was now mysterious, and Beth found herself enjoying everything as she waited for Dragon.

However, the second month was not as exciting. The days went slower. She found herself slipping back into boredom. Every morning her mother would again have to wake her with a sharp call. Beth would go downstairs and do her chores wearily, then head back to her room to stare at the parchment instead of playing in the lane. And while everyone else looked for the snows to come, Beth looked fretfully for Dragon.

Sometimes, though, she would slip away to the woods behind her cottage. There she would gather piles of sticks to make into dragons, with sharp branching claws and shriveled leaves for spines and rocks for heads.

"When will Dragon come?" Beth asked a stick dragon one morning as a crisp frost chilled the air around her. It was the driest winter she could remember, more like autumn with the leaves still falling slowly to the ground.

"I don't think Dragon is coming," she announced suddenly, hoping the stick dragon would tell her she was wrong.

The pile of sticks didn't answer. She sat glumly on the ground wondering if Dragon was only pretend. It was hard to keep faith in the message when days became weeks. And yet Dragon couldn't be pretend. She had the parchment. She could read it again and again. Yet why was there never another message from Dragon, explaining the delay?

"Dragon has to come!" Beth said firmly to the sticks. "She even sent a special messenger. She even..."

The girl stopped a moment and stared at the rocks that shaped the head of the stick dragon. "I said *she*..." she mumbled. "Yes, Dragon is a she. I know it!" Beth jumped up with surprise. "Somehow I know it."

Suddenly all Beth's doubts faded. She danced around the stick dragon as if it was Dragon, herself. "You are there. I can feel something. You are there," Beth said. Then she ran back to her cottage and sat in her room all that day staring at the message Dragon had written, knowing soon Dragon would come.

The next day, the snows came. They were strong and deep and killing. Herders lost their sheep. Traders lost many teams of horses and wagons caught out on the road. The storms kept coming. People fell into snowdrifts and froze or became sick and died. Beth's family lived in the kitchen of their cottage so, with only one room to heat, their supply of wood would last.

As the weeks went by, Beth found her spirits dragging. She had no hope of seeing Dragon now. Nothing would come in the storms. She would stare at the fire in the hearth, counting the weeks until spring. Sometimes, during a break between the storms, she would slip outside and carve into the wet snow the silhouette of a dragon.

It was early one evening, while storms clouds were advancing with yet another blizzard, that Beth carved one such dragon. After she was done, she warmed her hands inside her shawl and stared at the snow dragon for a long time. "I can't wait," she whispered to the dragon. "Please come. I can't wait."

All at once she heard a question rise inside her. It was her thought, and yet it was not her voice. "What will you do when I come?" it asked simply.

Suddenly Beth felt the same exhilaration she had felt when she danced around the pile of sticks. "I heard her!" she called to the snow dragon. "I heard her voice inside me! Someday soon she will come!"

And yet night after night, as the snows came down, Beth wondered how to answer the question Dragon had asked. "I will jump and dance and sing when you come," Beth would tell Dragon in her mind. Then she'd add anxiously, "Is that the proper way to act with a dragon?"

Finally, the snows stopped. The weather warmed, and Beth's family moved back into the rest of the house. Beth would lie at night beneath her quilt, holding the parchment, and dream of that moment when Dragon would come. What would Dragon be like? How would it feel to meet a Dragon? Would it be terrifying? Would it be grand? Would she really dare to jump and dance and sing before a dragon? Eventually she decided she had no idea what she would do when Dragon came.

The hills began to turn green. Beth didn't hear the voice again. All the questions inside her were her own. She could only stare out the window at the soft spring rain, wondering why Dragon didn't come now that the snows had gone and the roads were clear for travel. And, now, when Beth thought of seeing Dragon for the first time, she felt a troubling shiver inside her.

The days grew longer and less interesting. Often she would forget her lessons or her chores and slip outside to a meadow in the woods. There she would find some soft earth, wet from the spring rains, and form a huge muddy ball of clay. Slowly she would shape the clay into a dragon, and as she worked, she would speak to it, wondering if it in any way resembled the real Dragon.

One day she shaped a ferocious looking dragon with vicious claws and sharp cruel teeth. "Are you Dragon?" Beth asked as she stared at the gruesome face. There was no reply from the clay dragon so she continued watching the face, imagining meeting a dragon like this some day.

All at once Beth felt that shiver deep inside and she knew suddenly, she was afraid. How could she, Beth, stand before a dragon as fearsome as this? Beth knew she didn't have the courage to face a dragon. She hung her head in shame.

"Yesss," came the voice—Dragon's voice—inside her, "I can only come when you are no longer afraid."

Beth laid the clay dragon down by the stream. She sat quietly beside it. This time there was no exhilaration upon hearing Dragon's voice. This time her feelings were heavy for now she knew why Dragon didn't come. It was not Dragon that caused the delay. It was her. Wearily, Beth wondered why it had taken so long to understand the fault was hers, because she was afraid.

Weeks passed as spring bloomed around her. However Beth didn't feel the joy of sunshine and flowers and rain. Instead, she felt a great despair. There was no hope to see Dragon until she could conquer her fear. Yet she didn't know how to not be afraid.

The weeks turned into summer, hot and warm and dry. Beth was growing quickly. She seemed to be taller and stronger every day. She was strong enough, now, to work the bellows on her father's forge and, more and more, her father asked her to help him.

She hated it. The fire and the noise scared her and the heat of the shop made her sweat. She couldn't refuse to help, for her father would punish her, but when she was through she would run to the stream in the woods and splash into the creek to feel its coolness wash against her face. Then she would lie at the edge of the forest and stare at the clouds in the sky.

Often they were dragon clouds, great long gray wisps stretched high across the sky. She watched them all summer long, wondering if she could ever face Dragon. Then, as autumn approached, she went out one evening after a long day at the bellows. A great dragon cloud reached its wings wide. It seemed to hover above the fire of the setting sun, reminding her of the glowing coals of the forge.

Suddenly, Dragon's voice was speaking in her, "I am heat. I am flame. I am fiery breath. I am Dragon."

Beth's eyes opened wide. She saw herself at the forge, working the bellows, doing what she hated. And then, as she imagined Dragon rising from the forge flames, she realized how the heat and the noise of the forge were so much like the dragon she feared. Now she knew the way to learn to welcome Dragon.

So, all autumn she worked with her father, growing strong and comfortable with the heat of the forge. The bellows became her companion, like a baby dragon whom she taught to breathe its fiery breath. The glowing coals of the forge became Dragon's eyes, watching her with approval.

Then it was a day in winter. The clouds of storms crept across the sky, bringing with it the threat of snow. Beth went to bed that night feeling tired after her day at the bellows. She slept dreamlessly until early morning when she heard a scratching at the shutters. A rough, hoarse voice whispered,

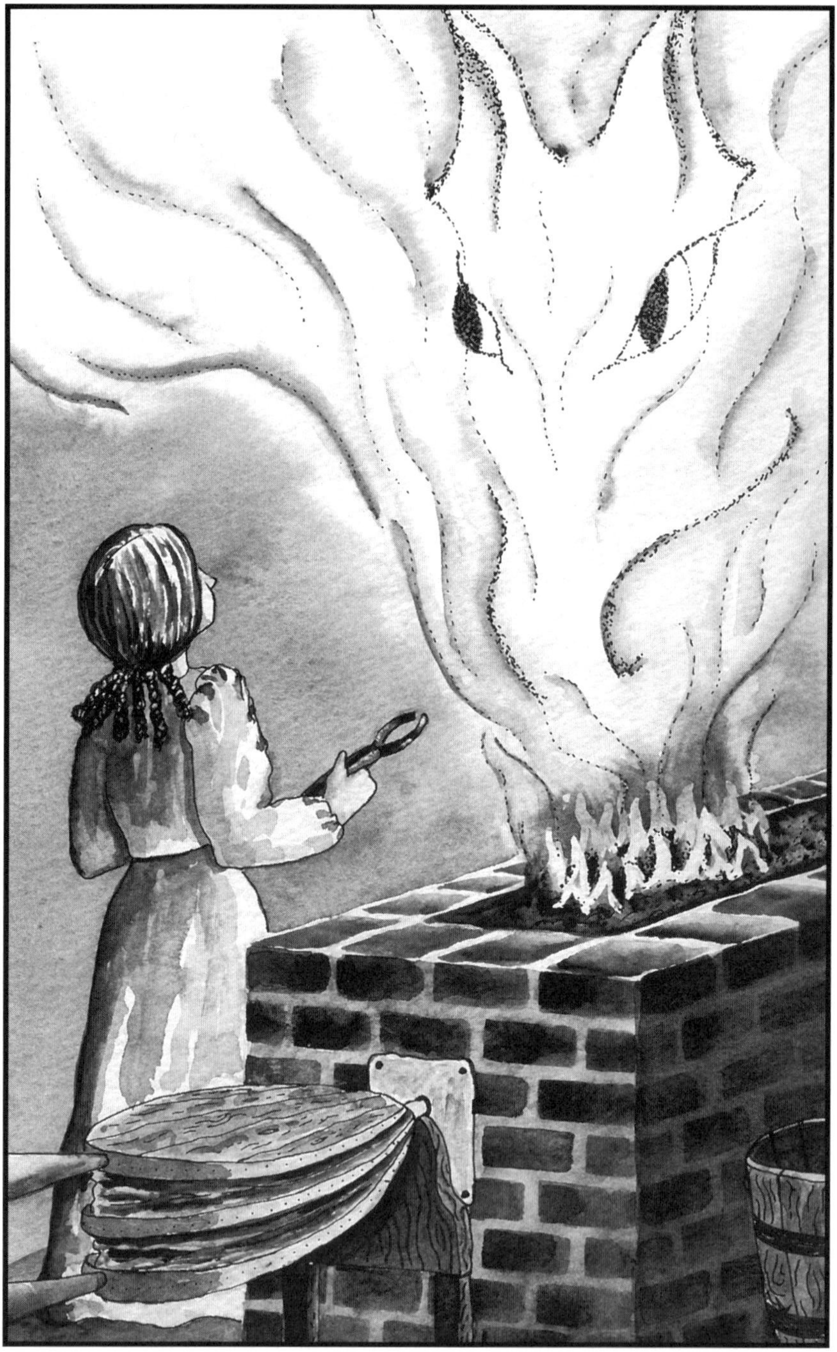

"Bethsss. Bethsss."

Beth rose in the cold darkness. She opened the shutters wide. There was the lizard creature with another scroll. She took it and opened it to the soft dawn light. "It is time," she read in a voice filled with awe. The message was signed like before: *Dragon.*

Quickly she dressed and went downstairs where the lizard was waiting in the lane beside her home. She followed it to a hill beyond the town. There they waited side by side as Beth shivered in the cold. Then all at once, there was no cold. There was only the warmth of dragon breath washing her shivers away. She looked up into Dragon's eyes as the great gray beast hovered above her. Those eyes were powerful and filled with fire, but Beth didn't cringe.

"Oh, Dragon," she whispered. "At last you could come."

Dragon landed beside Beth. With a hiss of flame roaring through her pointed teeth, Dragon nodded. "It has been a long time to wait. I'm glad, at last, I could come."

Beth studied the magnificent creature who looked more ferocious than any dragon Beth could imagine. The spines on her back glinted razor-sharp. Her claws were long and curved and strong as steel. Her breath felt hotter than the forge, and the eyes of Dragon penetrated deeper than any eyes Beth had ever seen. And yet Beth was glad to be with Dragon.

"Why did you come?" she asked.

"Because you wished to speak with me." Dragon answered simply.

"Yes, but before… when you sent the message…" Beth hesitated. "Why did you send the message?"

"You asked for something more in life," Dragon rumbled. "And I am something more."

Beth laughed out loud. "Yes, you are something more."

Snowflakes began to fall. A storm whistled around them. The two ignored it. Instead, they talked for hours—of dragon lore and magic in a world far beyond the village—while Beth stroked the lizard creature at her side lovingly. Dragon asked Beth questions about her life, too. As she answered, with Dragon listening intently to every word she said, Beth felt for the first time that she was interesting.

Finally, Dragon called to the lizard creature, "It's time to go."

The lizard climbed the dragon's tail and curled up near a wing. The dragon rose into the sky. Beth's heart ached to see her new friends go.

"Will you still watch me at the forge?" Beth called out hopefully.

"Yesss," Dragon answered.

Beth looked at the huge fiery eyes. "And will you come again to talk with me?"

"Yesss." Dragon winked.

Beth felt the power of the wings beating the air above her. "And someday, will I fly away with you to see your other world?"

Dragon spat a fiery breath and nodded. "Yesss."

"Then I'll wait," Beth shouted triumphantly. "For however long, I'll wait." She watched the dragon disappear into the thick clouds of the storm. Then she turned toward the village. "And this time," she whispered happily, "I know how to wait for Dragon."

A TIME OF WILLINGNESS

Long ago in the Valley of the Bells, a great sickness swept through the households of the tiny kingdom year after year. It struck only the young, and parents lived in despair, not knowing if their children would ever wake up from the feverish sleep they fell into. No one knew what sickness it was or when it would end, but one young girl, Kyra, knew she had to find a way to heal it. She had to—not for her sake but for Michael's. Michael had the sickness, now, and soon his life might end.

It was late-afternoon, the day after Michael fell ill with the fever, when Kyra ran up the lane from her home to the narrow canyon above her village. There, she climbed the tall rock beside the waterfall in the gorge and sat facing the breeze. This was the Canyon of the Miracle. The legends said that, long ago, people came from all over the kingdom to this very place to ask for miracles. And though no one believed the legends anymore, Kyra came to this ancient place determined that if miracles were ever real, they would be real again for Michael.

Not knowing what she must do, Kyra kept very still as if listening to the water. Yet Kyra couldn't hear the water as it pounded the rock, just like she could not hear the leaves rustling in the wind. She was deaf, and though she sat intently, she would never hear anything.

What Kyra could do was feel the softness of the breeze against her cheek. She could see the leaves moving and she could watch the spray of the waterfall swirl with the current of the wind. Every so often, a strong gust would bring the swirl of spray closer so the mist would wet her hand. She could feel the spray and see it, but though the world could touch her, it was forever silent.

Last year the sickness took her hearing from her. There was the fever and a terrible pain within her head. Her throat was swollen and her ears inflamed. But, after days and days on her sleeping mat, the fever broke. It spared her life, but left her deaf.

Before the sickness, she had worked by her mother's side, shaping bells for the village. Her mother was a gifted bellmaker, and Kyra had shown a talent just as strong. But now the bells were silent and Kyra felt completely bitter. What good was a bellmaker who could not hear bells ring? There were many times she wished the fever had never left.

Yet, now on the rock, feeling the breeze and watching the glory of the sunset wash the canyon rocks with red and gold, Kyra felt a hope within her. Perhaps her life had been spared a year ago for a reason—for Michael. Even though he had the sickness, she knew she wouldn't let him die. She loved Michael and she would find a way to save him, for Michael had learned to read and write when she went deaf.

Michael was the only child in the village, besides her, who could write or read. Other children were like silent ghosts that drifted through her life. She didn't know them anymore and couldn't hear their games or songs or what they said.

Michael was different. Together, they could laugh and have long conversations, writing with chalk against the small slate stone that she carried with her wherever she went. Together they could play games and build castles of rock and sand. Together, they were friends.

So, Kyra sat on the rock and thought of Michael. She knew she would give her life for Michael, she loved him so much. She longed to trade places with him on the straw pallet where he lay so hot and silent. She wanted to give him the chance at living that she'd been given a year ago.

Kyra trembled with her longing, like a bell that had been struck. Its chime was her feeling, so intense it seemed to echo through the canyon. Silently, invisibly, powerfully, it bounced off the rock walls and swirled the mist and shook the trees.

Then Kyra felt something on her arm. It was wet like the mist but it gripped her. She looked in alarm to see a shimmer of spray outline the fingers of a hand. She could barely see it as it tugged on her. It was powerful, and at first she fought it, knowing that the cold swirling water lay below. Then, thinking of Michael, she let go.

Suddenly she was pulled into the mist. The force of the waterfall struck her face, knocking her breath from her. She gasped and gulped and swallowed water. Then, just as suddenly, she was lying on the rocky ground soaking wet.

Kyra looked up into darkness. The first thing she saw

was the silver-green shimmer of the waterfall. She was behind it now. She could feel its force through her bones, pounding the rocks beneath her. She let her fingers soak up that feeling of power, like thunder in her hands. Then she felt a shiver in her spine and turned around toward the darkness behind her.

Peering into the shadows, she realized she was in a shallow cave, not much deeper than a small room. The dazzling brilliance of the waterfall was reflected in pools of light all around her. They seemed to glow among the shadows that filled this place she was in. Then she saw one pool sparkle more intensely and, within that pool of light, she saw the bell.

There, in the sparkling glow, was the most beautiful bell she could imagine. It was clear, made of crystal, but looked as liquid as the water of the falls. Resting on a rocky pedestal high above the floor of the cave, it was long and slender, with delicate lines engraved into it like the swirling mists behind her. Slowly she rose and walked toward the splendor of the bell.

And then a hand gripped her. It was the same damp hand that had brought her beneath the waterfall. She closed her eyes, waiting for the force of the water to crush her as she went back through the falls. However nothing happened, so she opened her eyes again.

Before her stood a man taller than her, but almost invisible in the gloom of the cave. He seemed to swirl and sway as if he were made of mist. He was dressed in a tunic of tiny drops and his outline glowed softly like the pools of light around them. Kyra stared at him in wonder. Then she realized he was speaking to her, but she could not read his lips.

Instinctively, she grabbed for her slate and tried to write

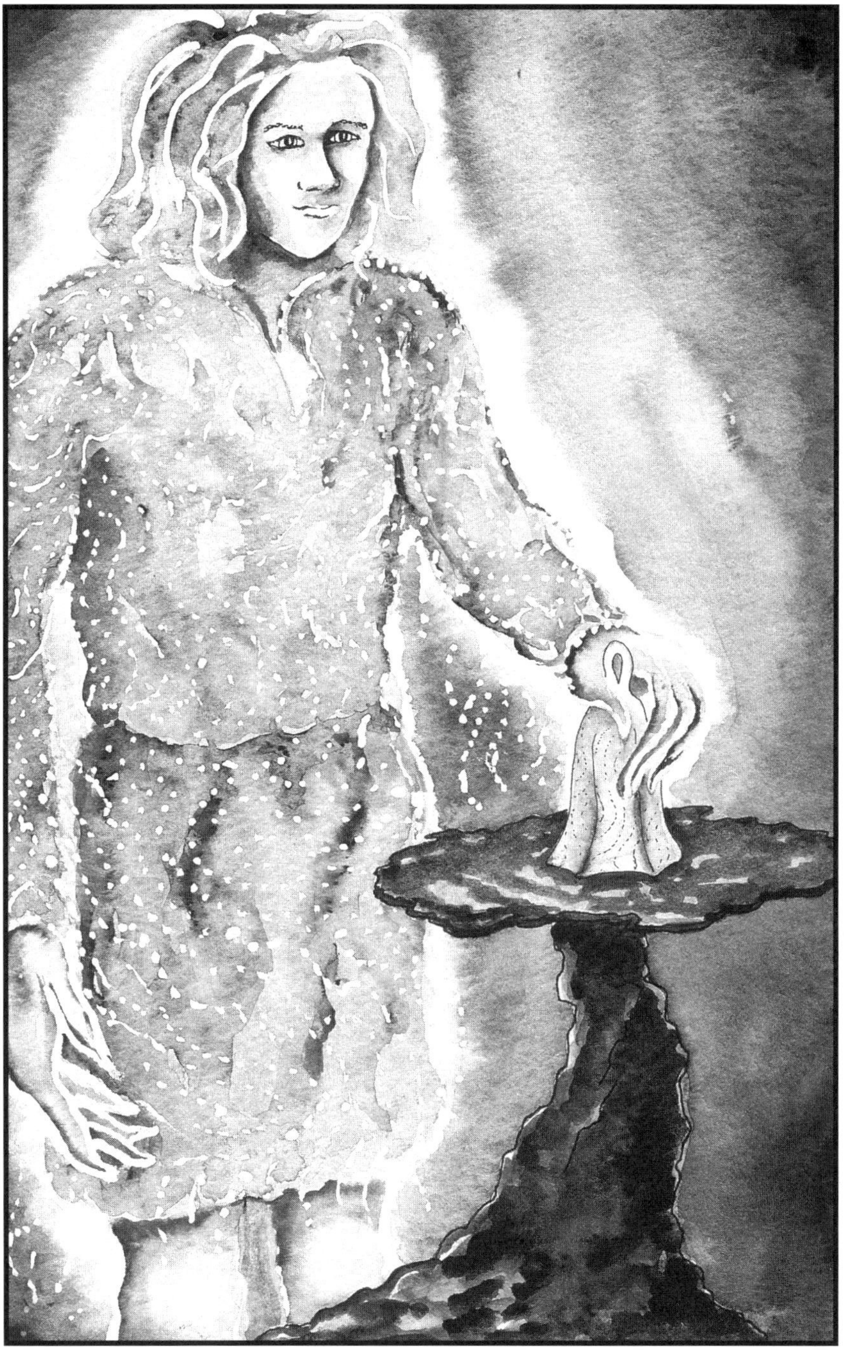

with her chalk. However the chalk was wet and it crumbled in her finger tips. She looked up at the man and shook her head in dismay.

He smiled at her. Then, reaching with a long arm that stretched like a wisp of spray, he touched the slate with his fingertip. Words appeared in a glowing script: *Welcome. You have come for the miracle.*

Kyra's heart leapt. That's what she needed—the miracle! She looked up enthusiastically and nodded. The man pointed toward the slate.

There was a new message which read: *The bell is waiting for you to sing.*

Kyra stared at it puzzled. Then the message changed: *You must offer the miracle to Michael. You must be willing. You must sing.*

Kyra looked up at the man confused. She hadn't sung or hardly spoken since she went deaf. It only made her feel frustrated, not knowing if she said anything that made sense at all. She could feel the vibration in her throat but not hear the sound. People didn't seem to understand her. And if she tried to sing, it would probably sound off-key. Yet, for Michael, she was willing, but what must she sing?

He pointed once more to the slate: *You must sing the note of the bell.*

Still confused, Kyra felt herself being pulled by the man toward the bell. She balked. She looked at the bell. It was so beautiful, but she hadn't touched a bell at all since she had lost her hearing. It was too painful, knowing she could ring it and not hear the beautiful note it gave. She shook her head. There must be another way for the miracle.

The man dropped his hand, waiting as Kyra struggled with her feelings. In her heart she knew there was anger and fear and grief for herself, but there was also love for Michael. She wasn't sure which one was strongest, but she knew which one must win. Kyra looked at the man of mist with hope in her eyes and nodded. Then, together, they stepped toward the bell.

The man picked it up with those long wispy fingers and gave it to her. Kyra felt the bell's gentle vibration in her hands. It must be ringing, now, as she held it, but she could not hear the note. She could never hear the note.

She looked back at the man. He looked dimmer now. The whole cave looked darker. The pools of light were gone. Kyra looked out toward the water. Its brilliance had vanished. There was darkness beyond. Kyra knew it was night.

The man touched her arm again and then the slate. She looked at it. It read: *You need not be ready, only willing.* Then it slowly faded. Kyra looked up. The man stepped back into the rock and was gone.

Kyra stared at the bell. It still glowed with its liquid light, but everything else was dark. Except for the pounding of the waterfall, which she could feel in the rock through her feet, she might have been anywhere.

You need not be ready, only willing. The words from the slate echoed through her mind. Kyra didn't understand. She could never be ready, for she could not hear. Yet, for Michael, she was willing for anything—for the miracle.

So she stared at the bell in her hand and felt its gentle vibration. She didn't know what to do. "I am willing," she thought. "I am willing."

Nothing happened. She didn't really expect anything to. Still she repeated to herself in her mind, "I am willing. I am willing. Whatever it is, I am willing."

And then she felt Michael stir in her heart, as if he were

breathing there. She felt the ache in his limbs and the fever hot and dry in his head. And as she felt him deep within, she also felt the gentleness of the bell rise through her fingers to her arm. It quivered like a spasm. She couldn't stop it. It spread to her shoulder and her neck. Her throat ached, like a gentle burning within. She took a breath, a deep, deep breath, and then she was singing. She could feel her lips tremble. And, with joy, she knew it was the note of the bell.

All at once, her whole body shook as if the waterfall was pounding her like the rock. She felt that note pouring from her, as her heart seemed to split wide open. She saw Michael's face, so clear in the darkness, and then she saw more—a girl's face and a boy, a little baby and another girl. They all could hear her in their fever, singing that note she could never hear. As the faces came, the note continued—delicate, yet powerful as love.

Soon, it seemed, that the whole cave was filled with a thousand faces and still she let that note flow through her. There was no need for breath. No strain. There was nothing for her to do, but let the singing happen and feel the joy of the miracle.

The faces came. The note continued. The crystal bell quivered in her hands. There was no way to know how long she sang and there was no need. Then, all at once, the pounding of the waterfall became still. Her throat stopped trembling. The bell felt quiet and there was a flicker of something—a stillness so deep it went way beyond the knowing of her mind. It passed so quickly that she might have overlooked it. And yet she could have never overlooked it, it was so profound.

Suddenly, she felt dirt and stones beneath her feet. She found herself on the lane, far below the waterfall, gazing up at its silent beauty. It was silver now in the light of the moon that was rising, and the shadows of the night only made the water seem more brilliant.

Kyra looked down at her hands. They were empty, but her heart was filled with peace. She turned, walking toward the village, thinking, not of the bell or the man of mist, but of Michael and the other children—all those faces she had seen.

Was Michael well? Were the others? She knew that would be answered by something way beyond her own desire. And yet, she felt she needn't hurry back to the village, back to Michael, to find out.

She looked gratefully at the waterfall. Her cheeks overflowed with her smile.

No. She needn't worry about Michael again.

MAMA ETA

There once was a girl named Bree who dreamed of ink and quills and parchment. She longed to use them just for the joy of writing words, her words, whenever she pleased. She lived with her uncle in a small crossroads village where they ran a tiny flour mill, earning only enough to buy their necessities. There was never money to spare for parchment.

All year long, Bree helped her uncle run his mill and dreamed of the day she would have all the parchment she desired. Her work was not hard. Uncle Jeno was a simple old soul who loved to sit for hours, watching his great grinding stones crush the small grains of wheat into soft fine flour. He didn't ask much of Bree except to have her open the water gates each morning, sweep the mill each night and set out his supper. So, for many hours of the day, the brown-haired girl had nothing to do but walk the hills above the village and imagine the stories she would write someday.

Often, though, as she wandered the hills thinking of her stories, she would be distracted by the whistle of a panpipe lizard or the scream of a screech cat. And sometimes she would forget about writing altogether and spend hours listening to the humming of a singing pony or the melody of a trumpet bee. Her village was at the edge of a vast, unexplored wilderness, called Aria, that lay beyond the borders of her kingdom. Bree was intrigued by the strange creatures she found at the edge of the thick, mysterious forest.

For years, Bree had longed to explore deeper into that wilderness of Aria, but she always returned each day to sweep the mill floor and set out her uncle's supper. She never had the courage to go there alone. However, one day, as she stood on the forest edge, she heard a sound she could not resist. It was filled with so much life and joy and beauty that Bree had to turn toward it immediately. She cocked her head and strained her ears to catch that sound of deep and hearty laughter. And then she crossed over the border into the forest and followed the voice.

After a lengthy hike, she discovered that the laughter was coming from a cave. Inside it looked dark and ominous. The opening was rather small and the tunnel beyond it looked even smaller. She didn't want to go inside, yet as she listened to the sound of that laughter, she knew she must.

The tunnel grew narrower as she inched along, but the laughter drew her further and further into the cave. Finally she saw a light ahead, and as she squeezed through a tight bend in the tunnel she came out onto a ledge. She blinked at the brilliance of a blazing torch on a wall beside her and gazed out into the openness of a great hall. She rubbed her eyes and sucked in a long breath.

There before her were dragons!

Three were small, about the size of a large horse. They were gray with a shimmering tint of color on the edge of their scales and wings. They sat in a semi-circle, gazing intently at a huge black dragon that almost filled the room.

The black dragon had ten centuries' worth of wrinkles creasing her face, but still she was an exceptionally beautiful beast. Each coal black scale was tinged with red. Her eyes, her wings and the spines along her back gleamed silver. A strand of sparkling diamonds hung from one ear and one gigantic ruby gleamed from the center of her forehead. Bree could not take her eyes off her.

"But I don't understand, Mama Eta," one of the little dragons whined from below. "How do I make the words come out?"

The black dragon opened her mouth and let out another hearty laugh from deep in her belly. Then in a raspy voice, filled with strength and goodwill, she replied, "When a dragon tells a story, they feel with their heart, listen with their mind and breathe very deep. Then the words come."

Mama Eta closed her eyes. She took a deep breath and was very still. The little dragons watched her in awe. Suddenly, the mouth of the great dragon opened. Out came a hundred puffs of smoke. To Bree's complete surprise, each puff was a letter and the many letters rose together to form word after word.

Bree leaned forward over the ledge straining to decipher each word as they drifted toward the ceiling of the cave. They formed a sentence which read: *Once, in the great dragon hall of the Grand Story Master, there was a girl hiding on a ledge, listening as three little dragons moaned about their lessons.*

And then, as Bree finished reading, she looked below

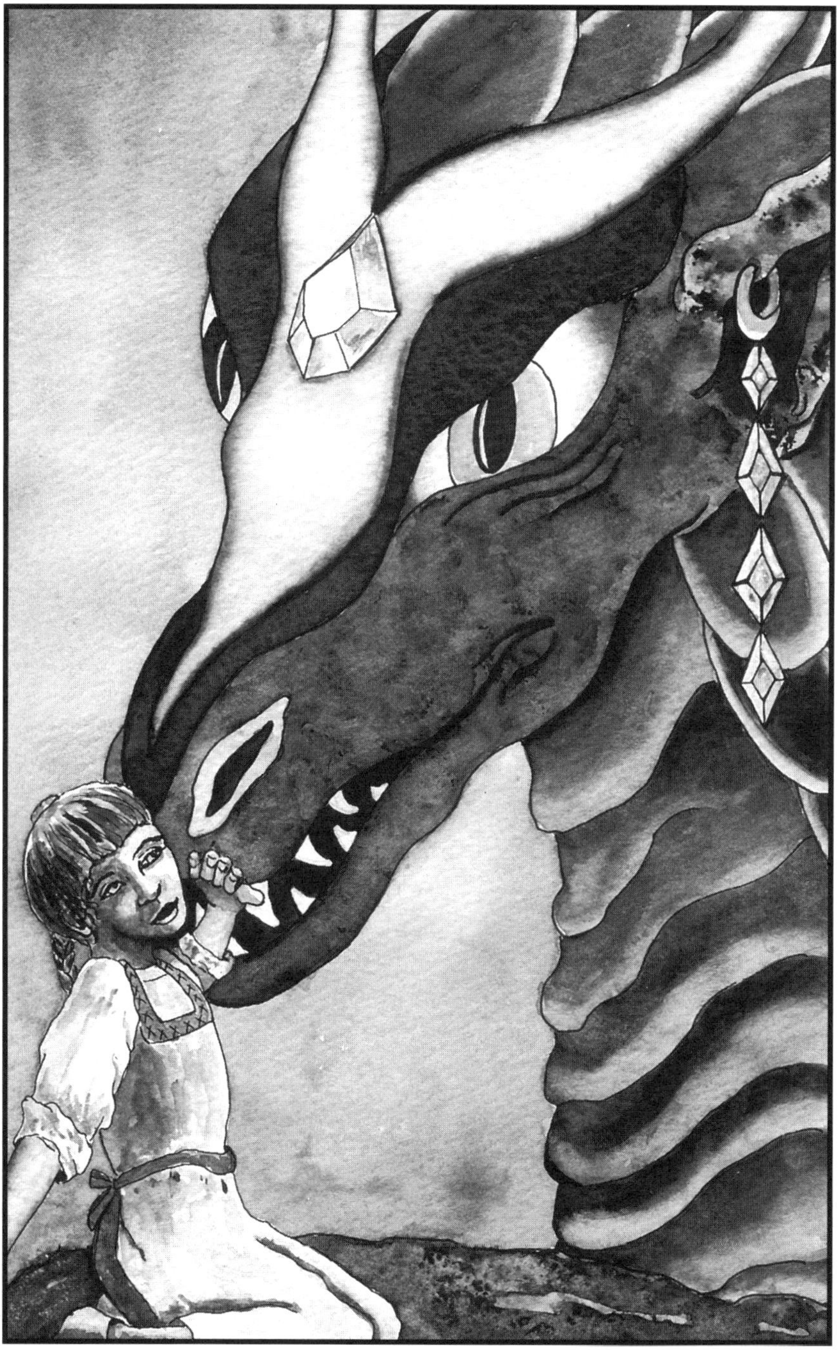

her. There were four dragons staring at her intently.

"Mama Eta!" cried a little dragon. "What is it?"

Mama Eta just let out a hearty laugh. "It is a human, my dear. A very small one at that."

The huge dragon stretched out her neck and raised her head to meet Bree's gaze. Bree shrunk back in terror. "I did not mean any harm," she sputtered.

Mama Eta blinked a silver eye. "Oh, but you have entered the hall of the Grand Story Master. Only students may come here."

Bree shook her head. "I'm truly sorry," she assured the dragon. Then she added hopefully, longing to know more about this wonderful dragon, "Perhaps I could be a student! Perhaps that's why I'm here."

Laughter, so thunderous that Bree had to cover her ears, filled the cave. It echoed down the many tunnels and corridors that ringed the hall. When it finally stopped, Mama Eta took a very long breath. She said calmly, "A human as a story master? Don't you know? Humans can't write stories. They have no fire in their breath."

"Yes," agreed Bree, "I can't write like you, though I wish I could. When I write I use parchment."

"So you are a writer." The dragon nodded with approval, but then she added cautiously, "But what do you write? You are human. You have no discipline to your mind. How do you shape the words?"

Bree shrugged. "I imagine them and then I write."

Mama Eta brought her face close to the girl. "Ah! But do you take responsibility for them. Do they become your life?" the dragon questioned.

"My life?" Bree frowned.

"Yes, when a dragon tells a story, it is the story of their

life," Mama Eta explained.

Bree's frown deepened. "Humans tell pretend stories, for fun."

"Just as I thought," Mama Eta said with a shudder. "Humans don't take charge of their lives. To be a story master you must write the words that build your life."

The girl shook her head. "I don't know what you mean."

"Of course you don't. You are human. You let life happen to you and blame everyone else when things go wrong." The old dragon rolled her silver eyes. "You are unteachable."

"NO!" Bree shouted. "I can learn! Please!"

Mama Eta looked at Bree thoughtfully. She blinked a silver eye. "Very well, human. Come down and take out your parchment."

With that, Bree withered on the ledge. "I have none," she mumbled miserably.

"And why is that?"

"I have no money," Bree whimpered.

"And why is that?"

Bree looked sullen. "I'm just a child. I have no way to get money."

"No," Mama Eta corrected her. "You are human and you do not write the stories of your life."

The black dragon raised her head to the ceiling of the cave. She looked down at Bree as if she were about to strike the girl off the ledge. Then the old dragon opened her mouth and let out one of those wonderful laughs that filled Bree with such joy. "Yet perhaps you will provide some motivation for my little students here. Perhaps you should join the class."

Bree looked up at her and nodded. Then she reached for the torch beside her and blew it out. "Oh, Mama Eta, I'm not unteachable. Look, I can write my words with this blackened torch. I can use a rock for my parchment."

Mama Eta grinned a sharp-toothed grin. "Perhaps you will become a story master after all."

And so it was that Bree became a student of Mama Eta, the grand story dragon. Every day Bree would open the water gates for the mill and then rush off to Mama Eta's cave to sit upon the ledge and listen to the great dragon's laughter. Everyday, the girl watched for hours as the three little dragons, Goldy, Perletta and Skymar, moaned and complained about their lessons. And everyday, Bree struggled to get even one word written on the stone to Mama Eta's satisfaction.

"You form the letter too quickly. There is no meaning behind it," the dragon scolded her gruffly. "It is too easy. It would be better if you had to shape the words with smoke."

"But I can't make smoke," Bree said forlornly.

"Then tomorrow I will bring you something else to write with." Mama Eta winked a silver eye at the girl and laughed long and deep.

The next day, Bree sat anxiously on the ledge while Mama Eta explained the chemistry of dragon smoke to the three young dragons. Goldy yawned as she stretched her gray wings, watching them shimmer with the faint hint of gold. Skymar rubbed his pale blue tail spines against a rock restlessly while Perletta tapped her dull white claws together in agitation. Finally the little gray-white dragon blurted out, "Do we have to remember all this?"

"Certainly not." The grand dragon lady chuckled. "You may stay my students forever if you wish."

"Oh, what misery," Perletta grumbled as Mama Eta continued with the lesson.

It was many hours until the lesson was done and each of the little dragons had shaped one small *O* with their smoke. Then Mama Eta turned to Bree. The girl's heart beat with excitement as the dragon deposited a sack on the edge of the ledge. "Open it," Mama Eta commanded.

Bree pulled at the string wrapped around the bag and then groped inside with her hand. A moment later she pulled out a stick. "What's this?" she wondered.

"It looks like a stick," Mama Eta said with amusement.

"But I can't write on stone with this," the girl protested.

"Are you sure?" the dragon lady challenged her.

Bree tried scratching a circle into the stone ledge. Nothing happened. She looked up at Mama Eta, waiting for an explanation.

Mama Eta winked at her. "It will take time," was all she said.

And it did take time. Months passed. Lesson after lesson would come and go as Bree sat on the ledge with her eyes closed, dragging the stick against the stone.

"Breathe deeper," Mama Eta would say. "You do not feel the word."

"But I'm trying," Bree would argue.

"You cannot force it," Mama Eta would advise. "It must just happen."

"Yet nothing does," Bree would whimper.

"You must focus and not focus at the same time," the grand dragon would tell her firmly.

And then Bree would sigh and continue, not knowing at all what the dragon meant.

One morning Bree woke with such a heavy feeling in her heart, she decided not to go to her lessons in the cave of Mama Eta. "It's no use," she mumbled.

She opened the water gates and watched the stream surge into the channel toward the wooden wheel that turned the mill stone. Slowly the wheel began to spin as the water was caught by the wooden blades on the wheel, pushing it forward—blade by blade, again and again.

Bree stayed by the wheel all morning, watching it turn. Uncle Jeno was surprised to find her there. "Are you sick girl?" he asked with concern.

"No, Uncle," she smiled up at him. "Just a little tired today."

"Take the evening off," he said generously. "I'll sweep the mill myself and fetch my own supper."

"Thanks, Uncle Jeno," Bree answered numbly.

It wasn't until midday that she began to regret not being at the dragon's cave. She wondered what the little dragons had learned today—whether Goldy had finished her second verse, or Perletta had finished her wish list. Skymar had been making great progress on his third smoky paragraph. Bree wondered how it had turned out.

Then, absently, she picked up a stick and began to drag it along a stone in front of her. Dreamily, as she watched the mill wheel turn, she practiced writing words. And when she came to the letter *O,* she found herself going around and around with the stick in rhythm with the wheel as it turned.

After a moment, she glanced down. There on the stone was the letter *O.* She blinked once and it was gone, but she didn't let the vision escape her. She held fast to it, as she jumped to her feet and raced through the forest to the cave of Mama Eta.

The dragon's grand laughter washed over her in warm welcome as she crawled through the tunnel to the ledge above the hall. All the dragons looked up, expectantly, when they heard her panting above them.

"Mama Eta!" Bree called. "Look!"

Then Bree sat down and drew an *O* on the stone with her stick, thinking in a clear but dreamy way of the roundness of the water wheel as she drew it. Mama Eta stretched her long black neck toward the roof of the cave and peered down at the girl, watching intently. When Bree opened her eyes, the dragon shouted proudly, "I see the *O*! You have learned!"

Bree looked down in wonder at the momentary *O* drawn against the rock of the ledge. "I felt the letter," she said with pride.

Mama Eta nodded. "You gave it meaning. Now do the same, writing with the torch."

And so, that very afternoon, Bree began to let her words become her life. Her first word was *parchment*. Her second word was *quill*. Her third word on the ledge was *ink*. Each word was written with the soot of the blackened torch, carefully and in stillness, as in her heart she knew what the word would bring.

That evening, before she left, Mama Eta presented her with a gift of a silver quill and a gold pot of ink. "The parchment you must get for yourself," said Mama Eta warmly. "But I don't think you'll find it so difficult anymore."

Bree smiled up at the huge face of Mama Eta. "It will be easy now," she said simply. "Thank you."

"It has been my pleasure," the grand dragon lady bowed her head slightly. "You were a very dedicated student. I will miss you."

"Oh, no!" Bree cried out with alarm. "I would never think of leaving."

Mama Eta laughed deep in her belly. "I cannot teach you

any longer, child."

"But I have so much left to learn," Bree said earnestly. "I haven't even written any stories."

"The stories you alone must feel—through your words," Mama Eta whispered gently. "A dragon knows nothing about humans and their stories. I cannot teach you how to write them."

Bree stood on the ledge fighting against the dragon's words. Then all at once she laughed. It was a belly laugh, not as loud, but just as deep as Mama Eta's. It spilled over the great hall in little echoes as Bree connected with some wise knowing waiting in her. She stared up at Mama Eta's silver eyes and winked, seeing endless possibilities she had never dreamed of before.

"Oh, no, you are mistaken. You can teach humans to write their stories." She bowed respectfully. "Don't you see, Mama Eta? You already did."

She picked up the torch and wrote on the rock ledge, very slowly: *There once was a girl named Bree who visited a beautiful black dragon whenever she pleased... and shared with her many stories.*

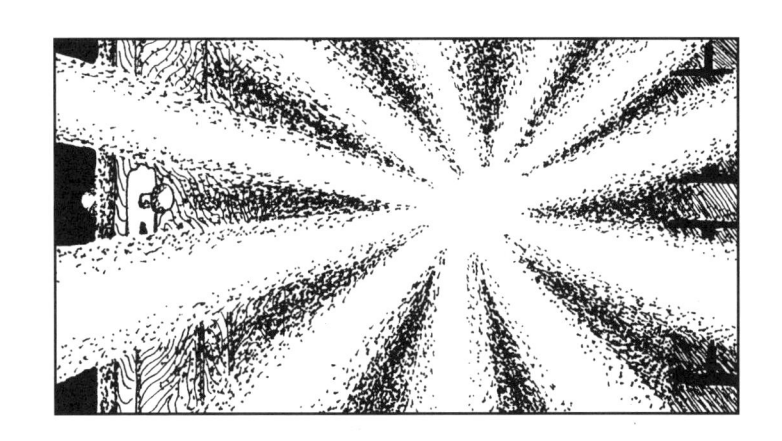

BEYOND THE DOOR:
REMEMBERING THE LIGHT

AWAKE AMONG WHALES

It was a night filled with starlight, or so the legend goes, when the whole sky burst with the brilliance of two stars arching towards earth. One star raced ahead as if it gleefully ran from the other. It gathered speed and fell to earth in the hills behind a small village. The other star took a different path, landing in some distant place which no one from the village could see. And in the village, on that very same night, the baby Celeste was born.

Celeste was the most active child the villagers had ever seen. She seemed bright beyond her years and could never stay home. As soon as she could walk, she sought out those in the village who did intriguing things such as the blacksmith, pounding red-hot metal, and the organ master, filling the whole church with unbelievable noise.

It wasn't long till Celeste, herself, was trying to do those very things. The organ master always let her play when she came to visit and once, when the blacksmith turned away from his forge, Celeste burned her finger rather badly trying to pound a piece of hot iron. There wasn't anything Celeste didn't try to tackle, but the thing she loved to do the most was to help an old man and woman map the stars.

The old man, Paul, had been a sailor long ago and had navigated by the stars. The woman, Juliette, knew the stars in another way—as myths and signs of the zodiac. Years ago, when Paul became too old to sail the seas, he came home to Juliette. Every clear night since, they would climb the hill outside the village to study the stars.

One night, Celeste and Paul gazed at the sky as Juliette told her favorite legend about a dragon who lived among the stars. And then Paul opened the wooden box that held his instruments. Juliette found her parchment and pen, and by the light of a lantern, they measured the heavens and made careful notes on the stars.

When they were done, Paul told stories of the sea. Celeste had never been near the ocean, but she pictured it in her mind as Paul spoke. She imagined the movement of the waves rocking her, and she imagined the cry of the gulls and the salty spray of the sea. However, all at once, she imagined something very unusual. She imagined a giant creature swimming in the water.

"Oh!" Celeste cried as she felt something brush past her. Then, in a moment, the sensation was gone.

"What's wrong?" Juliette asked.

Celeste shook herself. "I don't know. I was imagining the ocean. And then I pictured in my mind something large, something huge. What could it be?"

"There are some very large creatures in the sea," Paul answered. "You might have been thinking of a whale."

Celeste shivered. "But how would I know what a whale is? I've never seen one."

"Oh, I must have spoken to you of whales before," Paul assured her. "I've probably described one, and you imagined it, just as you imagine everything I say."

Celeste nodded slowly. "I suppose. But it seemed so real, I thought it had touched me."

Paul put a hand on her shoulder. "That's the blessing of a powerful imagination."

Celeste was quiet for a moment, staring at those twinkling lights above her. Then she asked, "Will you tell me again about the night I was born?"

"It was a glorious night," Juliette began, "cold and crisp. The stars seemed close enough to touch."

"And what happened?" Celeste prodded.

"And then two stars fell," Paul continued, "one after the other, like a mother chasing a child across the sky."

"One star fell near our valley and landed somewhere in the hills above the farms," Juliette added.

"But what about the other star? Where did it go?"

Paul shook his head. "Though we watched the other star to see where it would land, it seemed to disappear beyond the horizon. That's all we know."

Celeste sighed. "Someday I'd like to find someone who knew." And then she fell quiet, thinking of her vision of the whale.

Years passed before Celeste thought of whales again. In that time she had grown into quite a stunning girl. It wasn't that she was so beautiful. There were many girls more attractive than her, yet there was something wonderful about Celeste that drew everyone to her. At fourteen, she was courted by every young man in the village.

Celeste would have none of them. "I couldn't get married," she would tell her mother and father. "There's too much to do."

And Celeste did try to do everything she could imagine. Often it was something dangerous, like climbing the church spire or tracking wild boars across the hills. Sometimes she just had fun by playing hand rhymes with the younger children or dancing in the village square. There were still times you could find her in the stable helping the blacksmith with his forge. And at other times she worked with the village cobblers, carpenters, tailors and chefs.

However, Celeste could never settle on just one thing. Often she was rushing from one place to another, grumbling, "There's so much to do and never enough time." There were days you'd find her eating soup while painting a picture. And when she had to clean the house, she would read a book at the same time.

She spent less and less time on the hill with Paul and Juliette. First it was only once a month that she came. Then once every two. Finally, she saw them in the market one day after not joining them on the hill all winter long.

"Come with us tonight," urged Juliette. "It's the equinox."

Celeste sighed. "Oh, I've got three jobs to finish tonight."

"My goodness child," Paul grumbled, "what are you trying to prove? You run yourself ragged."

"There's just so much I want to do," Celeste explained.

"Except one thing," Juliette said soberly.

"Oh no. I want to do everything," argued Celeste.

"You want to do everything, except the one thing at the heart of you that you are trying to deny," Juliette advised her. "You would not run so hard, if there were not something you were running from."

Celeste fell silent. It had never occurred to her that there was something she didn't want to do. Finally she shook her head. "Oh, I'm sure that's not true."

Juliette touched her gently on the shoulder. "Just remember to visit us on the hill sometimes?"

Celeste gave her friends a hug. "Of course," she said. "Of course."

However, Celeste forgot about visiting her friends on the hill. She kept herself busier than ever. She planned her days so thoroughly that every minute she was awake was filled. Soon she resented all the time she spent asleep. To her it was time wasted.

Many nights, she would sew by candlelight till she fell asleep with the needle in her hand. Or she would sing, as she lay in bed, and no one in the house could sleep. But, finally, there came a night when she lay awake in the darkness and thought of the whale.

It had been a very busy day. Celeste had dug potatoes all morning, given an organ concert at noon, baked ten loaves of bread for a big family supper and danced till midnight in the village hall. When, finally, she lay down in the darkness to sleep, her mind churned faster and faster and faster, keeping her awake. All she could think of was a ship on the sea. She imagined the sails billowing with wind, and the waves crashing over the bow in a storm.

Suddenly, she saw a huge creature come toward her, like a fish, but giant in size. She felt the sensation of something brush past her, and then came its echoing voice. It was haunting and piercing and beautiful at the same time—fluid like the water and full of power like the waves. Yet the call of this huge creature was gentle and soothing and sure.

Celeste was startled. She put her hand to her lips. "Oh!"

she cried as she drew a sharp breath. Still, as if the song of the whale calmed her, she fell asleep.

Often, when she felt restless at night, the whale would come. First she'd see the ship on the water with waves crashing over it. Then she'd feel, very close to her, the sensation of the whale swimming through the water. Finally its song would fill her with a soothing, restful peace. More and more, when she lay awake in the darkness, she would hope the whale would come.

She also made time, again, for her old friends Juliette and Paul. Now, like the voice of the whale, she found the starry sky calming and reassuring. So, after a busy day, Celeste would walk with her friends up to the hill to watch the stars.

One night, the stars seemed surprisingly close. "I feel like I could touch the stars tonight," Celeste sighed. "Wouldn't that be great to be among the stars?"

"I often dream of it," Juliette agreed. "I often dream of riding comet tails and flying past the moon."

"But more than that, to be a star, to shine so bright, to be so... so..." Celeste searched for the word deep inside her. Finally she nodded and said, "To be so still."

"You think stars never move?" Paul asked.

"They spin I know, but they don't *do* things. They're not busy. They just radiate what they are," Celeste found herself replying. "Sometimes I would like to be like that."

"That could be boring for a girl like you," Paul frowned.

"Not necessarily," Celeste replied. "Not if you're a star."

That lofty thought did not slow Celeste down. By this time, she could play the organ better than her friend, the organ master. However her music never once would sound the same.

"You'll never be an organ master, my dear sweet girl," the

old musician scolded one day at practice. "No one can sing to music unless it stays the same."

"Oh, I couldn't be an organ master." Celeste shook her head.

"But if you don't marry, you must do something," the old man urged. "Perhaps you could write the music for others to play?"

"Yes." Celeste nodded. "I would like that."

And so it was arranged that Celeste would travel to a distant land to study music. Her dear friends, Paul and Juliette, volunteered to take her in her family's wagon to Lezure, a far off harbor town where she could catch a ship that crossed the seas. Paul was thrilled to go, to smell the salt air once again. Juliette was delighted too, to be able to share with Paul something he loved so.

They set off one autumn day in high spirits. Day after day, the three traveled as they talked and sang together. Night after night, they stopped at some cozy inn to get a meal and a room. And on clear nights, after a hearty supper, they always found a hill on which to watch the stars.

After many weeks, they reached Lezure and the shores of a great ocean. Celeste was overcome with joy. The waves, the gulls and the salty spray were all that she'd imagined on that hill back home. "Oh, Paul, don't you wish you could come with me on the ship?" she asked, thinking of the last part of the journey which lay ahead.

"Yes." The old man sighed. "But I have to get Juliette and this wagon back home."

"I could get home myself," Juliette scoffed.

"No," Paul said sadly. "The sea was long ago. Now it is the stars and Juliette." Paul took Juliette's hand and squeezed it.

Celeste smiled. "I will write a song for you, then, of the sea and the wind and the ship."

"A song like that would make me very happy," agreed her friend.

The next day Celeste's ship came into port and the inn was filled with sailors trading stories in their rowdy way. Paul spent his days talking with them happily, while Juliette and Celeste explored the town and the beach below. They were fascinated by the interesting things in the shops from far off lands, and delighted by the colorful rocks and shells they found on the beach.

One afternoon they walked clear down the beach to the headlands to explore the rocky pools at low tide. The little salty pools held the most amazing creatures—spiny urchins, slow-pokey snails and hilarious crabs encrusted with a bit of everything. Most wonderful of all, of course, were the brilliant orange starfish.

"Stars in the sea... I never thought I'd see stars in the sea," Juliette said thoughtfully.

Celeste nodded. "It's so strange. They cling to rocks like stars that cling to the earth..." she murmured, her voice trailing away.

Just then they heard someone scrambling over the rocks after them. It was Paul. He was waving and shouting and very excited. Finally he caught up with them. "I've just talked with the Captain," he said, puffing for breath. "Your ship sails tomorrow, Celeste!"

Celeste clapped her hands.

Paul grinned. "But I have more! Something wonderful! I was talking with the captain about the stars and I happened to mention that night, Celeste, when you were born. The captain knew the night I spoke of. He'd seen the stars,

Celeste. He'd seen those two stars and he knew where the second star fell!"

Paul paused a moment. Juliette punched him in the arm. "Tell!" she said firmly.

Paul winked at them and continued, "He was at sea that night, and the sky was clear. And he said, very definitely, that the second star fell—"

"Into the sea!" Celeste interrupted, strangely troubled. "The second star fell to the sea."

"At last you know," Paul said proudly. "At last we found someone who knew."

Celeste nodded and gazed out to the sea as if she searched those waves for something hidden beneath them. Then Juliette took her by the hand. "The tide's turning," the old woman said. "Time for us to get back."

The fog crept in very thick that night around the little inn. Celeste could not see from her window any of the lights burning on the ships in the harbor. But as she stared out the window, she felt like she was swimming through that grayness to somewhere, someone.

And then she saw the whale, swimming toward her, calling in that haunting way. It brushed her and the echoing call continued, like a song, punctuated with mysterious clicks and whistles and groans. She let it fill her as the whale circled, brushing her gently, till she caught hold of its tail.

Powerfully, she was pulled along through that foggy, unreal sea. Finally, they stopped in the middle of that watery grayness and everything was still. Only the sound of the whale, breathing through its blowhole, broke the silence.

All at once Celeste was aware of other whales near them. One by one they sent their spray of water and air above her as they exhaled. Then they were silent again, just drifting in

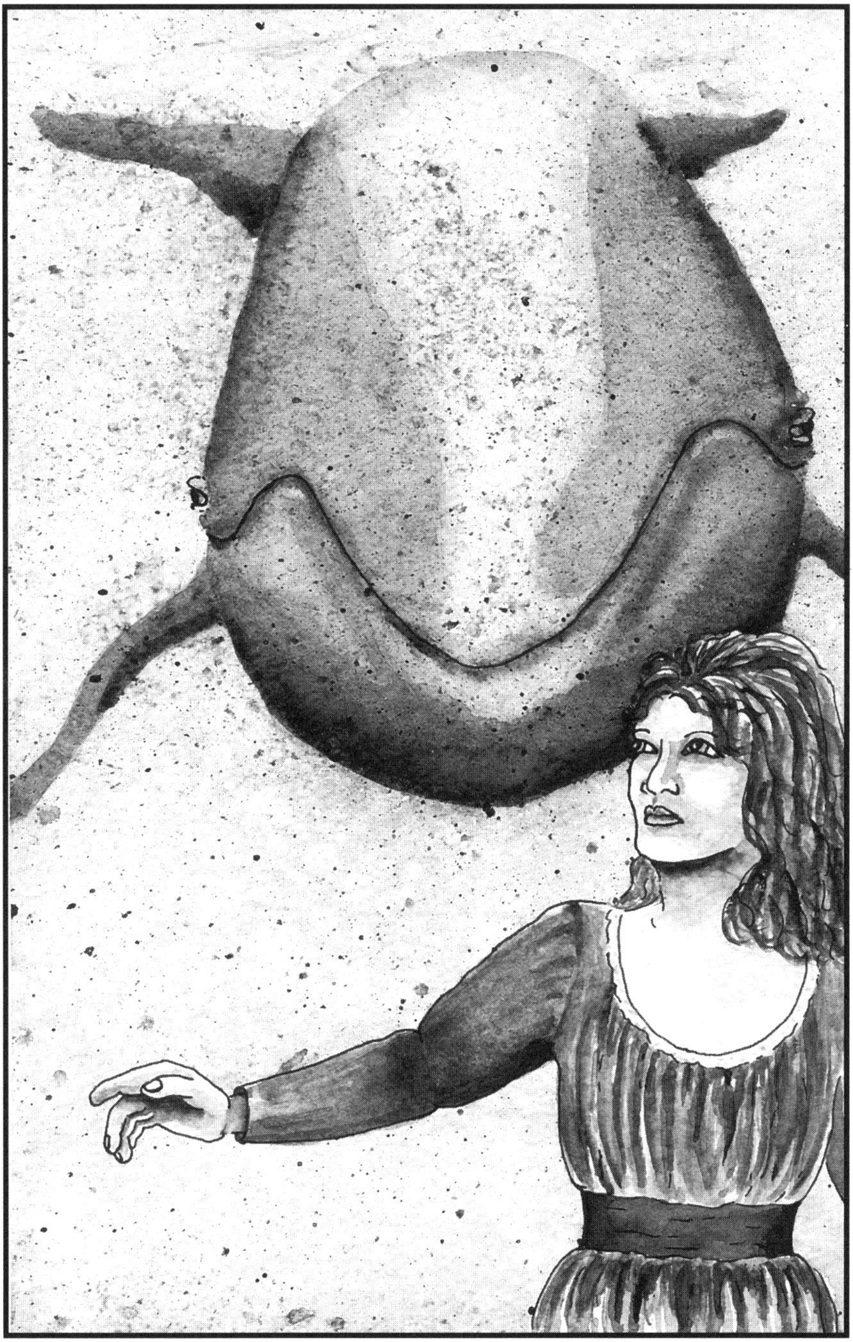

that gray sea.

A few whales began to feed, while some young ones frolicked. However most of the whales seemed content just to be still—just to *be*. Celeste realized how different these creatures were from people. They didn't spend all their time rushing, so busy with things. They didn't build or cook or clean. They spent their lives floating in oceans, gentle and peaceful and free.

Celeste closed her eyes and felt a longing deep within. She thought of the stars drifting through the darkness of the sky, so very much like the whales in the sea. She thought of something long ago that she couldn't quite remember.

And then the whale spoke. "Awaken, Celeste. Be with the whales. Awaken."

"Who are you?" Celeste whispered.

"You will know," said the whale, "if you stop all your running and *be*."

"Yes, that's what I've been doing," agreed Celeste. "I've been running. I've been running from myself."

"And," the whale added, "from me."

So, for perhaps the first time in Celeste's life, she let go as she floated in that grayness next to the whale. She felt her heart beat slow. She felt the rhythm of her breathing become steady and quiet. As if she had finally awakened from the nightmare of busy thoughts, nothing raced through her mind.

It was strangely quiet. She drifted slowly. A joy within her grew. The whales came closer, sensing her peace. She reached out and touched them one by one. Finally, after drifting with them for a long time, a thought came to her. It rang through her like a memory of her own voice repeating again and again: *The second star fell to the sea.*

All at once Celeste felt the speaking whale close to her.

She touched the thick, smooth skin gently. "You are the second star," Celeste whispered softly.

"And what are you?" the whale questioned.

Celeste felt tears in her eyes as she smiled at her knowing. Very quietly she answered, "I am the first."

Suddenly, the whales seemed to be moving off, and as much as Celeste wanted to follow, she couldn't. From somewhere in the distant grayness, she heard the whale call to her, "I'm here, Celeste. I'm waiting in the sea."

And then the little room at the inn was around her and the gray fog back outside the window. She was glad she was alone as she sat thinking of the whales. Finally she lit a candle and wrote on a piece of parchment the notes of a song. Then she blew out the candle and went to sleep.

When the foggy light of morning settled on her room, Celeste was already packed to go. She met Juliette and Paul for breakfast with the parchment in her hands. She looked at Paul and smiled. "It's not of the wind and the ship and the waves," she said. "It's of something more incredible. It's a song of whales in the sea."

The couple looked at her bewildered. Then Paul took it gratefully. "Whatever it's of," he said, "I know it will be beautiful."

And so Paul carried her bags to the ship as Celeste walked quietly beside Juliette. Then before she climbed the gangplank she hugged them both as hard as she could. "When you watch the stars," she whispered, "think of me."

Her ship set sail that morning through the fog, but it never reached that far off land. After a few days at sea, there was a terrible storm and the ship was lost. Celeste was never seen again by her family or Paul or Juliette.

Yet, so the legend goes, there were many sailors on watch

that night, on other ships beyond the storm, who claimed they saw a girl riding past them on the back of a whale. There was a pod of whales around her, jumping and breaching and slapping the water with their tails.

And there was one old sea captain who claimed the girl's hair glistened like silver even though there was no moon. He also said, as he watched her, she turned to look at him with eyes that sparkled like pure starlight. And he could swear, as they disappeared into the night, that the girl and the whale left the others behind—heading, not for the horizon, but the heavens above.

Though only the old captain saw her leave, many say that the sky burst with color all night long after the storm. The clouds parted and disappeared. The wind grew still. The stars shimmered blue and red and yellow. It was as if, the legend goes, heaven reached toward earth that night to welcome two bright stars coming home.

THE HEART OF THE DRAGON

Once there was a boy who lived among the dragons. His name was Dass and he was the dragons' keeper. He fed them each morning, cleaned their cave each evening and slept among them every night. He had done it for most of his life. That is why, unlike most people in his kingdom, he felt fairly comfortable in the company of dragons.

Still, Dass' parents had been killed by dragons, so the boy knew how dangerous a dragon could be. He had been raised by his brother, Sivar, who also lived in the dragons' cave. Sivar was the Dragon Lord and always cautioned Dass against the treachery of the dragons.

Years ago the dragons roamed the skies at will, burning fields and killing people. Then little Dass, when he was barely walking, found a ring deep within an ancient tomb. He was hiding there with his brother during a dragon raid.

The ring had power over dragons and kept them in their

cave. Sivar discovered this power and became a very important young man. He gave himself the title of Dragon Lord, believing that it was his duty to wear the ring and be the dragons' guardian. Year after year, those fearsome beasts stayed cooped up in the cave, plotting to steal the ring and be free.

"Why don't you ssstay and talk to me awhile?" hissed Moz, the old green dragon, one morning. He stared at Dass in a commanding way.

"You know I'm immune to your tricks." Dass laughed. "You can't stare me into a trance."

"It never hurtss to try," Moz admitted. "There iss nothing else to do."

Dass sighed. "It must be horrible, never seeing the sky beyond this cave. Even I get out once in a while."

"Oh, it iss horrible." Moz shuddered. "It iss. You must feel very, very sorry for uss and help uss escape." Moz said his words very slowly as he stared at Dass.

"You silly old thing." Dass chuckled. "For the thousandth time, I don't fall for your tricks."

Moz winked at Dass in a wicked way. "One never knowss," he hissed.

Then Dass picked up his feed bucket and went about his morning chores, thinking of the dragons.

"I wonder why the dragons are so terrible?" Dass asked his brother later that day. "It's a shame they can't get along with people. They're so magnificent. I'd love to see one in the sky."

"They look ferocious, not magnificent, in the sky," Sivar said severely. "I can tell you that."

Dass saw a look of pain cross his brother's face. "I'm sorry. I know I don't remember that day the dragons came. I just wish the dragons were different… then perhaps we'd still have Mother and Father."

That night, as Dass settled down to sleep among the dragons, he had a very odd feeling. He could sense something unusual in the cave. He looked around, always vigilant for trouble. However the dragons were curled up and snoring in their acrid, smoky way.

He counted them. "One, two, three, four, five, six, seven, eight, nine and Moz." Dass smiled at Moz. Moz was his favorite. He was a mischievous old fellow, with a wicked sense of humor, but Dass liked him.

Dass watched for a long time, then tried to sleep. He couldn't. He kept tossing and turning restlessly. Finally he rose and walked the cave. There was a winding tunnel in the rear of the dragons' chamber. At its end was a subterranean lake. Often Dass would walk the tunnel in the darkness and stare into the luminous glow of the lake.

Dass reached the lake quickly. He felt a strange urgency, as if something would happen soon. He walked clear around the lake and sat on its farthest shore. Then, as he stared into the lake's strange light, he saw something he had never seen before. It was a book, lying on a rock beneath the water next to him.

He reached toward it. He felt his fingers touch its cover. Then as he went to pick it up, he almost fell into the lake. Dass couldn't swim, so after he snatched the book from the water, he lay back against the wall of the cave with his heart beating wildly. It took a long time for his fear to fall away.

Eventually, he sat up and opened the book. The parchment was unlike any he had ever seen. It felt waxy instead of wet. He turned the pages. There were only a few, but they were beautiful—filled with fine pen drawings decorated with colored ink. Beneath each picture were ornate letters gilded with gold. The words were strange to Dass, but the pictures drew his careful attention for every one was of a dragon.

And yet the dragons in this book appeared much different than the dragons he knew. They looked like dragons, but something shone from their eyes. There was a softness there that he had never seen in a dragon before. It made the whole creature seem filled with splendor.

Dass studied the book for half the night. After he had looked over each picture, he went back to read the words. He couldn't understand them, but still he read them aloud. "Ushtar," Dass whispered as he read the first word. It glittered below the picture of a dragon whose wings were spread in flight. "Ushtar. Could it mean to fly?"

Opposite it was another picture of a dragon breathing fire. Beneath it was the word *Luth*. "I wonder if that means fire?" Dass asked himself. He turned the page.

The third picture was of a dragon eating from a large bowl. Below the dragon was the word *Megash*. Dass nodded his head. "Yes, it means to eat."

Next came a picture of a dragon, sound asleep. *Faroon* was the word below it. "Faroon is the word for sleep," said Dass with excitement.

The fifth page showed two dragons flying together. Dass read the words beneath the drawing, "Slurms ushtar." He shook his head. He didn't understand. But on the next page was a picture of two dragons curled together fast asleep. Its message read: *Slurms faroon*. Dass grinned. "Slurm means friend."

On the last page was a picture of a dragon's face. There was an incredible light in its eyes. Dass looked at the words. "Tura voka," he read. "Tura voka." Dass repeated it, again and again, but finally had to shake his head. There was no way for him to guess what that meant.

He closed the book. The cover felt smooth, yet stiff like leather. Then he noticed some faded letters that caught his eye. He studied them in the eerie light. "M, O, Z" he read slowly. He stared at the letters in disbelief. "M, O, Z? That spells Moz."

Dass felt his hands tremble. He dropped the book. A vision flashed through his head of the dragons, flying free. A gentle light shone from their eyes as they flew up toward the clouds through the sunlight. One dragon glanced back at him. He looked genuinely grateful. His eyes were filled with peace. Dass gasped as he recognized the creature. It was the green dragon, Moz.

Then Dass shook himself. "It's a trick," he fumed. "It's a dragon trick. I won't fall for your tricks, Moz." Then in a fit of fear, he picked up the book and threw it back into the deep, glowing waters of the lake.

Dass slept late the next morning. Sivar had to wake him up to feed the dragons. The dragon keeper rubbed his eyes. He yawned and stretched and stumbled toward his feed buckets. Then, as he approached a dragon, he threw her some meat and said quite unconsciously, "Megash."

Dass stopped and stared at the dragon. "Me... what?" the dragon mumbled as she gobbled her food. "What are you sssaying, Keeper?"

"Nothing, Kor. I didn't say anything," Dass murmured. Quickly, he turned toward the green dragon. "Moz, here eat."

"Thank you, Dasss," Moz said. "It lookss wretched."

"You are welcome, my slurm," Dass replied sarcastically. Then he blinked in confusion. He looked up at Moz, feeling very strange. He thought he saw something in the dragon's eye, like a soft light glowing. Then Moz turned away. The dragon hadn't noticed what he'd said.

After he had fed all the dragons, Dass hurried down the tunnel to the lake. He looked into the water. He could see the book there in the depths. However, no matter how much he tried, he couldn't reach it. He was too afraid he would fall in. Finally he sighed and sat beside the lake, trying to understand what the book and the vision had meant.

Eventually he fell asleep. And as he slept he dreamt of the green dragon, Moz. Moz looked younger and smaller, with that gentle light in his eyes. He was standing beside the lake and sniffling in a very childlike way. "I lost my book and I can't remember the words," he repeated again and again. Then all at once he looked at Dass. "Please help me remember. I can't remember," the dragon said.

Dass woke up with a start. He felt a gnawing emptiness in his stomach. He knew it was time for supper and chores, but he did not want to face the dragons. He was concerned they had some unexplainable power over him. Eventually, though, he hurried toward the dragon's chamber so Sivar would not come looking for him.

For a whole month, Dass avoided the dragons as much as a keeper could. Still, as he fed them and cleaned the cave, he felt the words from the book churning over in his mind. Then at night, when he curled up to sleep, he would look out over the great bodies of the beasts and feel a stirring in his heart and a longing to see them fly. And every time he looked into a dragon's eye, for a moment, he could see that soft light shine.

For a long while, Dass felt he was being tricked by the dragons and yet the gentleness of the light within their eyes nagged at him. He couldn't imagine how that light, which

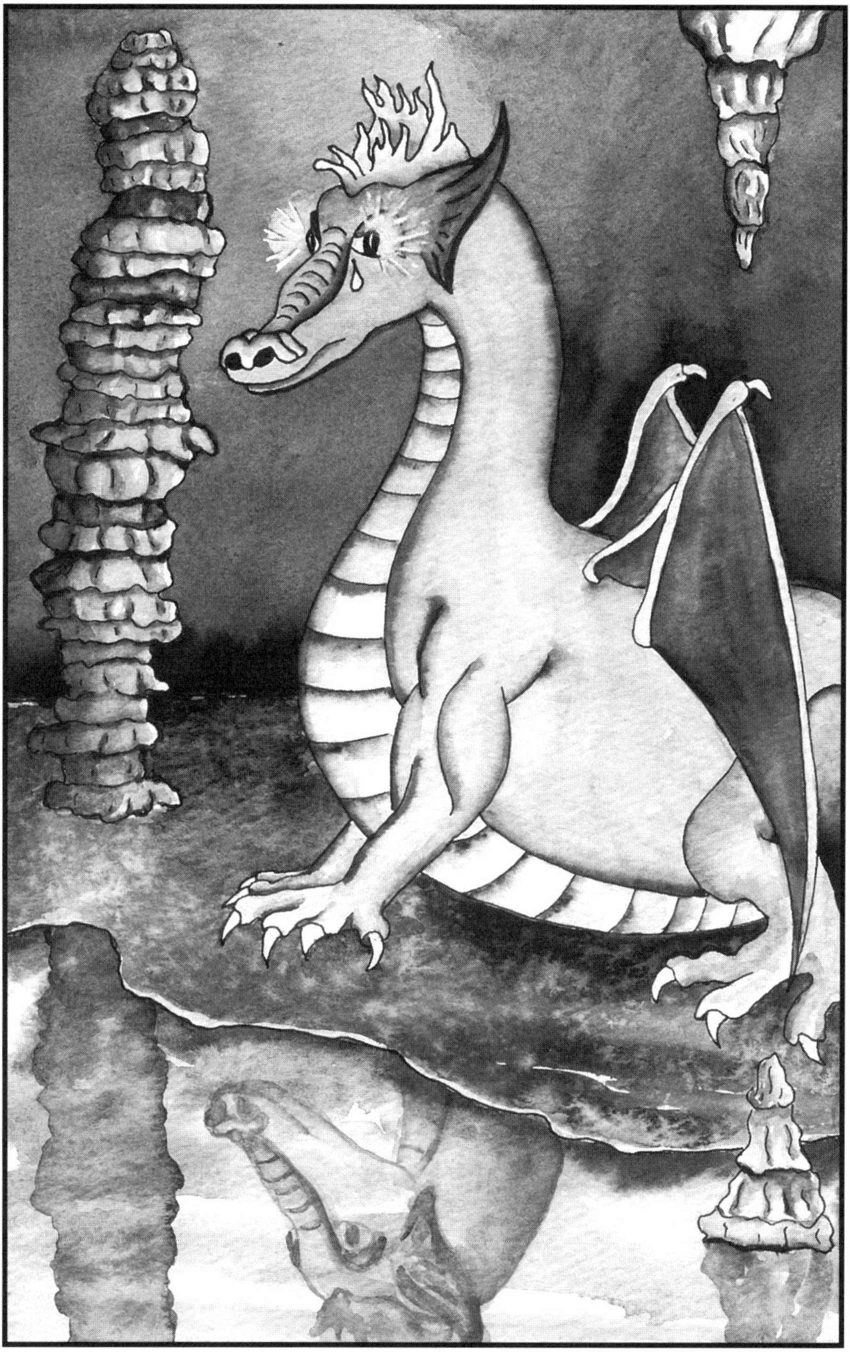

spoke to him of trust and kindness and friendship, could be conjured up by a treacherous dragon. And more and more, he became convinced that the dragons couldn't see it.

"Don't you notice how Kor's eyes shine?" Dass asked Moz one day while he was scrubbing out the cave.

"Shine? A dragon'ss eye doess not shine," insisted Moz. "It iss black like the heart of uss."

Dass studied the dragon. "I see a light in your eyes too."

Moz reared his fearsome head. "No need to offend," he hissed in pain. "I am your prisssoner. At least let me keep my pride."

Dass pointed to the bucket of water. "Perhaps it's just a reflection," he suggested to calm the dragon. But as Moz slithered away, Dass watched him carefully until he was satisfied that the dragon's reaction had been genuine.

Gradually, Dass became obsessed with the idea that the dragons might be different than they seemed. He let it fill his fantasies. He watched for every indication that a dragon might be good. And more and more, he sat and talked with Moz, listening to his stories as a good friend would.

Then one night, while watching the moon rise outside the cave, he imagined dragons filling the skies as they breathed fire among the clouds. But when he wandered back inside to do his chores, he overheard Kor, the youngest dragon say, "One day, we'll be free. Yess. Then they'll sssee what it means to keep a dragon in itss cave. It will be the battle of all battlesss. We will kill all the people in the kingdom when we're free."

For a moment Dass was very disturbed. This was why everyone feared the dragons. And yet he still felt, deep inside, they should be free.

He bit his lip as he swept the cave. Then suddenly, he

turned to look at Kor. She was a slender red dragon with a silver crest upon her head. As he stared at her, he imagined her eyes full of light, not just a tiny glimmer-full, but shining brightly like the dragon in the book.

All at once Kor noticed him. She looked at him and blinked. "Keeper," she hissed in irritation. "Go away."

After that, Dass spent a lot of time staring at the dragons. He would imagine them with eyes of light, doing gentle things or acting very wise. More and more the dragons became upset, till finally only Moz would speak to him.

"What are you doing that botherss everyone sso?" Moz asked him one morning.

"Oh, nothing," said Dass with a grin.

"They ssay you ssstare. Do you ssstare?"

"Sometimes," admitted Dass, "but in a kind way."

"If you wanted to be kind, you'd let uss go," Moz argued.

"It's not time. It may never be time…" Dass said with his voice trailing off. Then he stared at Moz, seeing in the dragon's eyes the light. Suddenly he felt a tremble in his heart. He reached out to touch the dragon tenderly. "Tura voka," he whispered. "Tura voka."

"What are you ssaying?" asked Moz, confused.

"Tura voka," repeated Dass. "What does it mean?"

"I don't know," Moz answered abruptly. Then Moz stepped back from Dass and slithered away.

The next day Sivar was called to a funeral. "It is a long journey, too long to take the ring. So here brother, you must wear it," Sivar explained as he handed Dass the magic ring. "I will be gone a week. Until I return, you must be the Dragon Lord."

Dass sucked in his breath as he felt the weight of the ring fall into his hand. He felt both dread and hope—hope that the dragons could go free, and dread that he might actually let them. "No Brother. Find someone else. I wouldn't be a proper Dragon Lord."

Sivar shook his head. "There is no one else. Just guard the ring. There's nothing more to do." Then Sivar turned and walked out of the cave, leaving Dass alone with the dragons.

That evening Dass didn't do his cleaning chores. Instead he hid in his brother's chamber at the mouth of the cave. He felt excitement soaring through his heart. He saw the vision of the dragons flying free. He also felt the ring, heavy on his finger, and wished his brother had never gone away.

Dass tried to busy himself with dusting his brother's books, but it was no use. It only reminded him of the book in the lake. Its words came crashing through his mind. "Ushtar. Megash," he found himself mumbling. "Faroon. Slurm. Tura voka." Those last two words became a chant. "Tura voka, tura voka," he repeated again and again and again.

Finally Dass put down the dust rag and paced the chamber floor. "Tura voka," he mumbled. "Tura voka… if only I could know what those words mean."

Suddenly he stopped in the middle of the floor. He pictured in his mind that last drawing in the book. The light of the dragon's eyes seemed to swirl around him. "Tura voka," he whispered. "What does it mean?"

All at once he found himself racing to the dragon's chamber. Moz was curled up ready to sleep. "Moz!" he called as he shook the dragon. "Tura voka. Tell me. What does it mean?"

Moz opened his eye. "Tura voka? I told you. I don't know what it meansss."

"But the book," Dass sputtered, "your little book… it was

written inside."

"What book?" asked Moz. "Dragonss don't have booksss."

"Come," urged Dass. "Come and look."

Finally the boy convinced the dragon to follow him down the tunnel to the lake. When they reached its shimmering shore, Dass peered into its water. "There it is. See it. Down there."

Moz followed the boy's finger with his gaze. "A book. Yess, a book. I've never ssseen that there before."

"But Moz, you must have seen it," argued Dass. "It has your name on it."

Moz stared into the water for a long time. His eyes were puzzled, as if he were trying to remember something, but he couldn't.

Dass watched the old dragon, looking for a sign of that light in his eyes. They were empty for a while. Then he saw it—a little glow, soft and gentle. "That was your book," Dass began. "You lost it long ago when you were young."

"When I wass young? I don't remember being young. That was thousandsss of yearss ago."

"Think! Think!" urged Dass. "It was a little book with pictures of dragons and words like ushtar, megash and faroon."

"Ushtar?"

"Yes, ushtar. It meant to fly. And megash meant to eat. And faroon meant to—"

"To sssleep!" Moz nodded triumphantly. "Faroon meant to sssleep." Then the dragon turned to Dass. "But how could I know that?"

"Because you knew when you were young, but you've forgotten," Dass explained. "And now it's time to remember. You must remember. What does tura voka mean?"

Moz stared at the little book. "Yess, I remember. Tura—it

meant pure. Voka—it meant heart."

"Pure heart!" shouted Dass. "Pure heart! I knew it. A dragon's heart is pure. You've just forgotten. Long ago, it was forgotten."

Moz shook his head. "No. Dragonss are not pure."

"Please remember," pleaded Dass. "Please remember what you are."

All of a sudden Moz spotted the ring on Dass' finger. "You wear the ring. Where iss your brother?"

"Yes, I wear the ring," Dass agreed. "My brother will be back in a week. Right now I have the power to let you go. First you must remember."

Moz stared at the boy for a long time. Then the dragon settled down on the edge of the shore and stared into the water. He spoke slowly as if seeing something far away. "It wasss a lesson book, I think. Yess. Then we did have lessonss. I lost it like you sssaid, that day, when the older dragonss flew out together and never came back. We were magnificent then, but people ssstill feared uss. They killed the older onesss, all our parentsss. Then we learned to fight back."

"And because there was no one to teach you, you forgot what you were?"

"Yess," agreed Moz. "We did forget."

"I'm so glad you can remember, but the rest, will they?"

"Yess," Moz decided. "I will help them. Yess."

Dass stared at Moz. The light in his eyes grew. Soon it was brighter than Dass had ever imagined. Moz stared back. "Ssslurm," he said. "Vaku."

"Vaku?" asked Dass.

"It meanss thank you," Moz answered with a gracious bow of his head.

Finally, they walked out into the large chamber full of

dragons. Dass watched them as they slept. In his mind they seemed transformed. They were gentle, magnificent creatures, who had merely forgotten that their hearts were pure.

All at once, Dass tugged on the ring. It slipped from his finger. He showed it to Moz. "Here, I give you your freedom. I cannot keep you any longer."

"But your people, they will kill you," argued Moz.

"They might," agreed Dass. "I never considered that."

"Then come with uss," urged Moz. "You have alwayss been our keeper."

Dass smiled. He felt bathed in the kindness of the dragon's light. "That's true. I have never been anything but the dragons' keeper. Yes, I will come. I would like nothing else but that."

The moon had risen full when the dragons left the cave. They spread out their wings and took flight, filling the sky with dragons. Many in the kingdom saw them and trembled with fear, but no one died that night from a dragon's fire or claw. Instead, the beasts circled once around the sky, as if to say farewell, then disappeared. No one knew where they or their keeper went, but when Sivar returned home he found a note from his brother.

It read: *Dear Sivar, I have gone with the dragons. Here is the ring. Keep it if you must, but I assure you, Brother, you need never again fear what lies in the heart of the dragon.*

THE ENDLESS LIGHT

Long, long ago, in the chilly stillness of a desert night, a girl named Larana crept to the rim of a canyon. Peering over the edge, she stared at the red stone temple below her. It looked alive with people, moving in and out, as it glowed magically in the moonlight. She shivered as she recognized the black robes of the guardians and thought of what could happen to children caught by them within the temple gardens. Then, touching the leather pouch that hung around her neck for reassurance, Larana gripped the trunk of a gnarled Seek-tree and let herself over the edge.

Inch by inch, she worked her way down the cliff, using ledges and crevices and trunks of the twisted Seek-trees as handholds and footholds. Each year the descent grew easier because she was taller and could stretch further. Yet there were still sections of the cliff that challenged her. She wondered, as she made her way over them, how she ever climbed down this wall of rock, the first time, when she was just six and so small. However, looking back, she knew nothing could have stopped her that night.

Larana remembered the deep pain she had felt six years ago as she watched her parents take her dying grandmother to the Temple of the Spring. She had screamed and fought and cried, begging her sister to let her follow and be by Grandmother's side.

"You're too young. They won't allow you near the temple," her sister warned. "And if they catch you, we may never see you again."

Larana knew what was said—that children found in the garden could be taken from their families and sent to work in strange places far away. She didn't know if it was true, but she had vowed to herself that she couldn't be kept from Grandmother. So, as her sister slept that night, she had run away into the darkness, searching for the temple.

Now, as Larana groped for each tree trunk and crevice with her fingers and feet, she wondered if it was indeed the same tree or the same crack that she had found the year before. Always it felt, year after year, like she was moving in a dream that kept repeating. Yet, as Larana stopped to look up at the moon, she felt the breeze cool on her cheek and she knew she wasn't dreaming. That was the wonder of it. All that would happen tonight and it wouldn't be a dream.

When Larana reached the bottom of the cliff, she stopped to remember the way through the gardens of the temple. She studied the shrubs and the flowers and the trees, almost overwhelmed by their variety. It was strange to walk among this lush growth after living in the bleak landscape above, day after day.

The temple was surrounded by a crystal spring. Its clear,

cool water nourished the gardens and was said to heal those who drank from it. Larana wasn't sure how many people were really helped by the spring, but many, including her parents, believed it did. That was why they had brought Grandmother here six years ago.

Grandmother had wanted to die peacefully in her home of stone and clay. She had lived there her whole life and wouldn't be moved. But as Grandmother's spirit slipped further and further from this world, Larana's mother decided to take her to the temple against Grandmother's wishes—and Larana's.

The tall grasses and ferns brushed her hands softly as Larana slowly made her way through the garden. Here the Seek-trees grew tall and thick, their needles bushy and long. She counted them as she walked, then turned left after the fifth one, remembering how she had hidden from a guardian that first night. She had waited till the guardian disappeared toward the temple, then circled around to the side to avoid others. There she had sat in the tall grass, peering into the temple, looking for a sign of her parents or Grandmother.

Larana sat in that same spot, now, peering through the grass toward the temple. The red stone columns were dark with shadow since the moon had moved toward the eastern horizon. However, the candles in the center of the temple cast ample light, letting Larana see the people within.

There were hundreds of people within those huge stone columns, washing themselves or their loved ones in the water of the spring. As Larana watched, there were some who left, smiling and seemingly better. Many, though, were carried away—just as feeble as when they came.

Larana drew a deep breath filled with the scent of Seek-trees. She thought of all she had learned in those years since she had first come into the temple gardens. If only those people could understand what she now knew about healing and about death. She had tried to talk to others, but none believed her, not even her parents. She was still young, they thought, and given to foolish dreams.

The people came and went. As Larana waited, she found herself thinking of Grandmother, years ago, working the red clay of the earth with her hands. Grandmother loved earth. She always said it was alive, and as she shaped her pots and jugs and platters, she sang to that living magic she felt forming in the clay. It was that magic, Grandmother said, that made her pots sell quickly. And it was that magic that Larana had sought to feel as she worked beside her Grandmother, molding the wet clay.

Larana touched that small leather bag around her neck, feeling the hard shapes within. She remembered that night, six years ago, as she watched the people in the temple, just like now. There had been a snap behind her as a twig broke under someone's heavy foot step. She had sprung to her feet ready to run, thinking it was a temple guardian. However, before she fled she caught the smell of wet earth and saw the lump of clay in someone's hands. Then peering through the shadows, Larana had seen the long, long braid that was Grandmother's.

Larana sighed with joy, thinking of that moment again and again. Then a temple guardian walked by, so close she could almost touch him with her hand. She sat as still as stone, letting him disappear into the darkness, listening carefully for another sound.

Finally it came. There was a swish in the grass behind her. Larana's body tensed, not with fear, but with expectation. She felt again that rushing exhilaration. She turned and whispered into the shadows, "Grandmother, I'm so glad you've come."

"Of course I've come, child," a low voice chuckled. "Of course I've come."

Larana's heart burst with feeling as she jumped to her feet and flung her arms around Grandmother's round waist. She buried her head in the heavy tunic that had taken on the smell of rich, wet clay. "A year is so long," Larana whispered, "so long to wait."

"It is not long... for what you're learning," her grandmother assured her.

"Oh, but I forget so quickly," Larana muttered.

"You will learn," Grandmother assured her again.

Then Larana took hold of the cord around her neck and lifted the small leather pouch over her head. She pulled on the gathers at its top to open it, then poured the contents into her hand. "What will it be?" she asked as she stared at the small clay shapes she held. "What should we make this year?"

"We have the moon, the star, and the flaming sun," Grandmother said as she touched the objects gently. "What are they for?"

"The Light," Larana answered.

Grandmother pointed to the last two pieces in Larana's hand. "The tree and the beetle, what are they for?"

"The Life," Larana replied.

"Then what are we missing?" Grandmother asked.

Larana hesitated. "Something more for The Life?"

"And what could it be?"

"A goat, a flower, or... or maybe you! It could be you, Grandmother."

Grandmother smiled. Then she added calmly. "Or it

could be Larana. This year let it be Larana."

"I'd much rather it be you."

Grandmother patted Larana's hand. "Remember, though, these are reminders to carry with you. I think it will be helpful to have a reminder called Larana." From her pocket, Grandmother took a lump of clay.

Larana stared at the clay, then sighed and took it from her grandmother. She sat down anxiously, feeling awkward for the first time since she had been coming to the temple gardens. She shook her head. "It doesn't feel right."

"I know. It's hard to include yourself in something so wonderful," Grandmother explained. "But don't deny the truth, child. Don't deny the truth."

So Larana began to squeeze the clay, working with her fingertips to mold it in the dim light. However, no matter how much she prodded the little lump, she could only get the crude outline of a person's body. It seemed to have no form.

Finally she set the clay down. Inside she had a queasy feeling, and when she looked up at her Grandmother, tears rushed to her eyes. "Something's wrong, Grandmother." She wiped back a tear. "I just feel terrible. It feels like the end. This is the last piece, isn't it? And when it's done, you won't come back."

Grandmother touched her shoulder gently. "That's true, Larana. I can't hide that from you. When you finish this piece, you won't need me to come here anymore."

"Then I won't finish it. I won't!" Larana took her fist and smashed the clay flat. She stared defiantly at Grandmother.

Grandmother chuckled. "I see. I guess our learning is done." Suddenly, the woman began to fade as if she was melting into the shadows around her.

"No," Larana begged. "Please. I'll… I'll finish the piece."

"That's better," Grandmother called from the darkness. "I suggest you just shape your face."

"I will, but come back first," Larana pleaded.

"Start first," came Grandmother's firm reply.

Larana sighed and nodded and picked up the flattened clay. She began by pulling out the little stones and stems of grass that had been imbedded in it when she smashed the clay on the ground. Then she formed an oval disk and slowly started to mold her face, all the time watching for Grandmother. Finally her beloved grandmother emerged from the darkness, flesh and blood again.

"I'm not sure this is me," Larana said pointing to the piece.

"Feel it deeply and it will be you," her grandmother assured her.

Larana took a deep breath and let its energy flow through her as if she were breathing into her hands. Her fingers tingled with sensation and Larana began to work the clay lightly, almost without thought. Finally she stopped. She looked up at her grandmother. She stared at her for a long time. At last she said sadly, "It's done."

"It *is* done," said Grandmother gravely, but with a twinkle in her eye.

"It's not funny," Larana argued. "You won't be back."

Grandmother smiled. "I won't be back," she agreed. "So, now you must learn to come to me."

There was a sudden rush of wonder and emotion that filled Larana. She put her fingers to her lips and laughed and cried at the same time. Then all at once she sputtered, "How? How can I? Must I die, too?"

Grandmother let out a laugh so loud, Larana expected a

temple guardian to appear any moment. Finally the round woman took a deep breath and wiped tears of laughter from her eyes. "No, my child," she said with a loving grin. "You have a long life yet ahead. But you can learn to penetrate what keeps us apart. It will take practice. It won't come quickly, but to start with, this time you hold the clay," answered Grandmother.

"Me?"

"Yes. You."

So, Larana stood before her grandmother, straight and tall, like she had for each of the past five years. This time, though, she cupped the small clay piece in her own hands instead of giving it to Grandmother.

Her grandmother looked at her with sparkling eyes. "So, Larana, tell me what you know."

Larana giggled self-consciously. Then slowly she spoke the words Grandmother had taught her, "The Light is endless... never broken. And The Light and The Life are one."

They stood silently for a moment. Larana stared at her Grandmother's face. A soft glow seemed to pulse around her aged, crackled skin. Larana looked to her grandmother's eyes. They were brilliant with light.

"Repeat it," urged Grandmother.

Larana stretched even taller and spoke more boldly. "The Light is endless, never broken. And The Light and The Life are one."

Suddenly her vision blurred. Grandmother's face stretched out of focus. The radiance of the eyes engulfed every feature she had come to love so well, until only shimmering light stood before her.

Larana braced her mind against the panic she felt each year when she saw her grandmother melt into this vision of

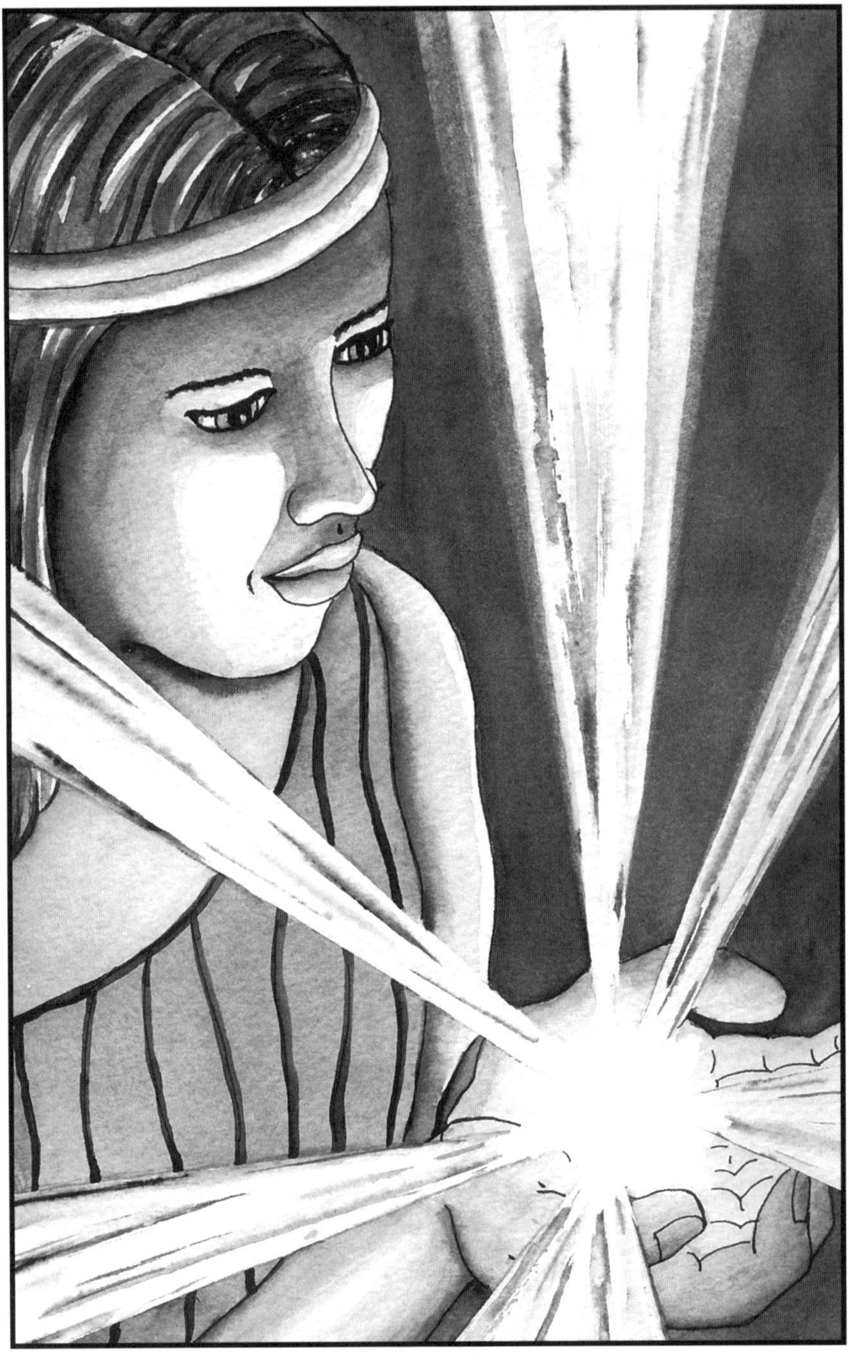

light. She focused on her breathing, keeping it slow and steady, as if she were making a pot and feeling for the magic in the clay.

"Repeat it," came Grandmother's voice from the pulsing glow.

Larana nodded, but when she spoke, her voice quivered strangely, "The Light is endless, never broken. And The Light and The Life are..." Larana felt her jaw tremble as she tried to finish the last word. She felt her hands grow hot.

"One," she managed to say as she looked from the pulsing glow of her grandmother down to her own hands. They felt alive with flame, but they looked normal. And then, in an instant, they were gone, replaced with that same brilliance that had consumed Grandmother.

For the moment, she was too shocked to resist. She had never imagined this happening to her. Grandmother was different. Grandmother had died—had gone beyond the body. But Larana knew that she, herself, was not dead.

Swiftly, that radiance spread up her arm, dissolving her whole body into its sparkling mystery. She became a light, which spread ever outward, and it was a light that Grandmother shared. Grandmother was no longer beside her, separate. They blended, one with the other, in that loving, gentle light.

Then, all at once, she heard a twig snapping in the darkness. She blinked and looked around. The light was gone and a guardian came toward her. She stepped back deeper into the shadows, letting him pass by as she searched the darkness for a sign of her grandmother.

There was none. Grandmother was gone. She was alone again and all she had to show for the wonder of those moments was the oval disk of her face still cupped in her palms. It was no longer moist and soft, for it had been baked in that living fire that had burned within her hands. She shivered slightly in the chill of the canyon, feeling somewhat awkward with her body, grasping for a shred of the understanding she had known just a moment before. It had slipped away, like Grandmother. Yet she knew it wasn't gone, for a gentle tremor of its peacefulness remained within her heart.

Larana picked up the pouch and carefully slid the oval of her likeness inside. She heard the piece clunk softly against the other objects and smiled. The set was complete. She no longer had to come to the temple gardens. Grandmother would never be here for her again.

She strode out onto the path toward the temple and the stairs that lay beyond it. She no longer thought to hide from the guardians. She no longer felt she should climb the steep rock wall to return home. Yes, they might catch her, but that meant nothing now. How could it, knowing that endless light of Grandmother's was hers to share?

She reached the temple stairs and began to climb out of the canyon. Guardians walked by her without notice. People passed her, with lines drawn deep into their weary faces, desperate for healing. She didn't stop until she reached the rim of the canyon. There she turned to look one last time at the temple. She touched her pouch and smiled.

"Little girl," came a man's voice behind her, "you cannot go to the temple. It is forbidden. It is only for those who need healing."

Larana faced the voice. She saw a temple guardian, standing watch at the top of the steps. He looked so solemn in his black robe. She stared at him, thinking of all she could tell him if he would only listen.

Finally, she smiled and then spoke with a boldness that

surprised him. "I have no need for healing," she replied. "Nor for the temple."

Then she stepped into the darkness of the desert night and was gone.